D1600608

THERE IS NO CLOUD

KAT WHEELER

There Is No Cloud

Copyright © 2021 by Kat Wheeler

Coordinated by: Hot Tree Self-Publishing
Editor: Hot Tree Editing
Interior Design: RMGraphX
Cover Designer: RMGraphX

Paperback ISBN: 978-0-578-82396-6

For Bob, who taught me everything I know about sales.

THERE

IS

NO

CLOUD

KAT WHEELER

CHAPTER ONE

THE SHORT LIFE OF MATTEO RODRIGUEZ

MATTEO Rodriguez was a tall man, so getting clubbed in the head to death was only possible because he was sitting down. Too bad being an IT guy didn't come with psychic powers, because that Friday evening, he wasn't thinking about it being his last night on earth. He was thinking about designing a new keyboard. A more ergonomic one for guys his size. Tucking his elbows in to hit the keys hurt after a while, and programming involved hitting lots of keys.

No longer called Matteo but Matt by his colleagues, he had developed the product that had taken Synergistic Engineering, already a giant in computer components, to a household name. Before Matt, Synergistic Engineering supplied components to computer manufacturers. Their cutting-edge processors were a necessity to all major computer companies. But it was his HomeTech Hub that changed everything for them. His Home Technology Hub and AI Information System, or HomeTech Hub (HTH) for short, had been a vague idea through his four years at MIT. It was also the subject of a paper he wrote in school. One that garnered the attention of tech icon Wilson Howell III, better known as Trey, the owner of Synergistic. It was widely speculated that at least one Synergistic component was in every PC manufactured.

What appealed to Matt most about going to work at Synergistic wasn't the money. It wasn't the ridiculously high salary Trey had offered him to start, although that felt good. It wasn't the ability to pay off his loans, which were once crippling, or to be able to help support his family. Although all those benefits were wonderful. It wasn't even having access to all the cutting-edge hardware Synergistic manufactured, stuff that would no doubt make it easier to develop his HomeTech Hub. What drew him the most was the kinship he felt with Trey.

The first time he met Trey was on the campus at MIT. He remembered wondering if the guy was lost. Most students on campus weren't exactly what you'd call fashion-forward. And this guy was *GQ* on steroids. He'd walked up, introduced himself, and started the conversation with flattery on Matt's climbing history, not his academic successes. And that's what reeled Matt in. A peer as into developing both the body and the mind as he was. A man who'd distanced himself from his family and was self-made, just like himself, albeit in reverse. It seemed on that first day, as they drank too many pints at Matt's favorite local pub and discussed his ideas for his great invention, that the future was nothing but bright and filled with possibility.

That was five years ago. It seemed Trey had changed since then, and if he were being honest with himself, Matt would admit he had changed too. It seemed success had affected them both. It was most noticeable to Matt here, in his office.

That night found Matt sitting where he always sat: his private office in the Synergistic building. It spoke to Trey's East Coast roots that he headquartered the company in the heart of New York City versus the typical Silicon Valley locale. Once the HomeTech Hubs had shipped and taken off in popularity, Trey set about constructing this space. He bought the building at 29th and Broadway in Manhattan. It was a far cry from the offices he'd started in with Trey. Though perfectly fine, it was nothing when compared to the grandeur of this monument to success that Trey had built in the city. Gleaming white and metal in every corner. Large screens everywhere, either for employees to use as huddle spaces or showing marketing videos of Synergistic's achievements. And technology everywhere. Everything was automated, even the coffee maker. Just press a button from your laptop, and in a few minutes, you could have whatever latte or mocha waiting for you in the break room of your specification. They often joked that it would only be a matter of time before Trey found a way to have it delivered to you. But as nice as it was, the opulence was becoming unbearable for him, and he longed for the simpler times before his invention had taken off.

Matt's office was three times the size of his first studio

apartment in the city. Despite his impressive salary, he was conservative with his cash, preferring to save more than he spent. But he had upgraded and bought himself a nice two-bedroom in a new building. Real estate in New York City was always a good investment, he told himself. He'd never been rich, and while appreciative, he wasn't quite comfortable with the money he was making. And slightly unsure of himself. Would it last? Would he be able to deliver the product he'd dreamed up?

He had delivered. Made all his dreams a reality and created the first real piece of consumer-friendly artificial intelligence. Deliverable to any home and natively integratable to whatever tech they had on hand no matter how it communicated. Bluetooth, Zigbee, Wi-Fi, Z-Wave, or thousands of other proprietary protocols with no coding required. He'd built all the applicable APIs in the cloud and could translate data from device to device in seconds. He'd cut through all the old technology infrastructure and developed a Rosetta stone to bridge communication and make technology magic. And it learned too. Learned what you liked to listen to in the morning, when you liked your shades up or down, what time you went to bed, woke up during the week, on the weekend. What you did during the holidays. So many real-life applications. It could track the weather in your location and perform daylight harvesting to save energy. Automate all technology based on your preferences on Shabbat if that was your thing. No more hiring expensive programmers to do it for you. The possibilities were endless. It could now happen natively.

And Matt Rodriguez had made it happen.

But the long hours over the years were starting to take their toll. Matt hadn't taken a vacation since college, and he could feel his dream of completing the Seven Summits slipping away into the daily grind. He'd long offered to teach Tessa how to climb, and that still hadn't happened. He thought he'd have time once the product started shipping. After the years of R & D, triumphs and failures, the HTH was finally on the market and selling far beyond their wildest dreams. It was estimated that over ten million homes and billions of devices were now connected to the HTH. But the release of the hub had not brought relief for Matt. Almost immediately there were intermittent reports of defects in the product. Matt and his team had been working on it since the initial shipments began rolling out last year. He'd been unable to point to the cause of the malfunction in certain units. Until now.

Yesterday, he discovered something in one of the returned units. Something that wasn't supposed to be there, and it terrified him. And that was why he was sitting alone in his office on another Friday night, waiting to report what he'd found. It would mean the immediate recall of all units on the market. They would have to stop shipping all product immediately. It was going to cost a fortune. Their stock was going to tank. Trey would not be pleased; they were going to lose everything. All those years, all that hard work down the drain. But he knew without a doubt it was the right move to make. The implications of the intrusion he found could not be ignored.

It was coming up on 9:00 p.m., and his meeting was already half an hour late. Not unusual. So Matt didn't even turn around when he heard the automatic door to his office slide open.

"You're late," he said to his visitor. "You need to see this and then get on the phone with all our factories to halt production. I know the implications, but this needs to be done. Something is wrong with one of the hubs. I can't understand how this could happen, but we must issue a recall, check them all. Make sure this is the only one."

It was then that Matt realized his guest hadn't spoken since they'd walked in, which was out of character. And they were standing uncomfortably close to his back. Matt began to turn around to address his visitor face-to-face when he felt the first blow to his head. As Matt's head fell onto his keyboard, the blows didn't stop, but he was beyond feeling them. He didn't see the killer reach over him to access his computer or crack open the CPU and remove the hard drive. While Matt lay dying, his killer slowly and methodically removed all evidence of his discovery. They grabbed the gear they'd removed and walked calmly out the door, and since everything was automated, they hadn't touched a thing.

CHAPTER TWO

SAME MEETING, DIFFERENT DAY

"I just can't keep sending guys on-site for this! Do you know how much it costs to send a team into the city for a service call? It's gas, labor, parking."

Cameron Caldwell was trying to focus on Barry's rant, but her eyes kept straying to the clock on the wall. It was 2:36 p.m. The clock was an old-school model that reminded her of Barry. Dusty and ancient and so out of touch with the modern technology they sold. She'd been listening to him go on for twenty-two minutes. She'd timed it. She was ashamed that remembering how to tell time in the old analog way had taken her more than a few minutes. She was so used to digital or just asking her tech what the time was. She'd been staring so long that she couldn't decide if it was her imagination or if she really could hear the tick, tick, tick of the second hand moving. Cameron had been a sales rep for SmartTech Home Automation for five years now and had heard this same speech from Barry more times than she could count.

Barry Issacs was an aging hippie who ran one of the most profitable A/V integration companies on Long Island. His client list was a who's who of hedge fund billionaires, musicians, Hollywood icons, and politicians. His office was a shrine to his vanity, with pictures of all his famous clients posed with his prized Harley-Davidson. She was embarrassed to admit her photo was on the wall as well. A visual reminder of the lengths she would go to for a sale.

It was to his benefit that he recognized he wasn't the most personable fellow and left all the sales to his partner, Adam. With his ruddy, jowly face and permanent scowl, he couldn't be the face of the company. But he was perfect for harassing his vendors and negotiating deals in his favor. He was making more margin on SmartTech products than anyone else in her territory. Mostly she caved on deals just to shut him up. She was fairly sure he knew it too. And that's what today was. He was going to keep on until he broke her. Until he got her to agree to take responsibility for a product she didn't even sell. It was going to work too. With every tick of the clock, she felt herself caving in. Trying to determine how little she could promise just to get the hell out of there.

She was an hour out of the city. If she left by three, she could beat most of the traffic on the LIE and be home in the city by five. It was a Friday afternoon, and she desperately wanted to be done with this week, back in her apartment with a bourbon. And she had her weekly call at four. Something she tried never to miss less she completely lose her sanity. Or whatever of it was left after a meeting with Barry.

"Barry," she interrupted, leaning forward in her chair. "I hear you. And I understand your frustration. No one likes to throw away money, but I don't know what I can do for you. We don't make the HTH. I can't troubleshoot products we don't manufacture. Have you tried calling their tech support?"

"Of course! We've spent hours going over this with them and your team! They say their HTH is fine. It's only failing when connected with the SmartTech control system. The units work just fine standalone. This customer paid me half a million dollars to automate his house, and I can't make a fifty-dollar HomeTech Hub integrate? It's ridiculous!"

"So where are we at right now? You swapped the piece out, and it's working?"

"For now" was his snide reply. "But we just replaced two last week. They connect and then fall off the network. I have two right here. Same model, sequential serial numbers, one works and the other doesn't. It's got to be your HDMI cables or your matrix."

"Barry, that makes zero sense," she replied, taking a deep breath and forcing herself to chill before responding, making sure to keep her tone calm and even. "If everything in the system is the same and the only change is the hub, it's got to be an issue with that. They're not even connected via HDMI. It's about your network. What kind of network are you using? Did you unplug and plug the router back in?"

"Cisco, and of course we did!"

"That stuff's solid, and if you've updated all the firmware and everything's current, it's not your network. You have defective HomeTech Hubs."

"I can't do any more of this he-said-she-said bullshit." His face had reached a deep color of purple, and Cameron began to worry about a heart attack. That would certainly keep her there way later than she wanted to be if she had to wait for an ambulance. She shifted again in the ancient, uncomfortable chair and felt herself giving in even as her ass was falling asleep.

"Barry, 99 percent of SmartTech systems have HomeTech Hubs installed with no issues. It's a problem with your hubs." He didn't blink or bother responding, just stared her down from behind his ancient wooden desk, and as she knew she would, she caved. She didn't have it in her to listen to the ticking or Barry anymore. She sighed. "Fine, give me the two HomeTech Hubs you took out, and I'll see what we can do."

Barry smiled a smug grin at her as he handed her the boxes.

"All I ask is you do the right thing. You're a good girl."

What a condescending ass, she thought as she left his office, but ass or not, he had won. Cameron vowed to herself to never schedule a Friday afternoon meeting with Barry again. It gave him too much leverage.

The drive back to the city loomed before her, and Cameron had plenty of time to think about the meeting she just had. She'd scheduled it to be an easy Friday afternoon planning Barry's Q2 sales forecast, but she should've known better. Nothing was ever easy with Barry. Nothing was easy with any of her clients since the HTH had been released. It was nothing but problems.

The Synergistic HomeTech Hub was a fifty-dollar voice-activated AI interface meant to introduce artificial intelligence into homes. AI was a trendy buzzword these days, even though anyone with any sense could tell you true AI didn't exist. But the reality was the hub was just a cheap piece of hardware. Among other things it was supposed to integrate with home automation equipment and learn to control it with your voice without anyone having to push those pesky buttons anymore. Verbal commands were the thing now. Cameron was an outside sales representative for the largest home automation company in the world, SmartTech. They manufactured everything you could want to automate your home: motorized shades, automated lighting, HVAC interfaces, and everything you could ever need for audio and video in the home. But that stupid hub was in almost every home in the country now, and Synergistic didn't offer much in the way of service and support for their products. The HomeTech Hub was systematically driving her crazy.

She had worked hard in her career, and at twenty-seven landed the prestigious territory of NYC, Long Island, and the Hamptons. If you were a sales rep in her business, there wasn't a better job to be had. Growing up in Kentucky was a big departure from the life she now led, living in Manhattan, selling luxury tech to the one percent. But she loved it. She loved the small one-bedroom apartment she had in Gramercy Park. She loved being within walking distance of so much stuff. New York truly was the city that never slept, and Cameron Caldwell thrived on it.

What she didn't love were people's assumption that because she sold technology, she was some kind of tech genius. No one assumed medical sales reps were doctors. Yes, she was good with technology. Software more than hardware for sure. But she wasn't an engineer. She also hated that people automatically assumed she was their go-to for tech support. She had to cut her mother off years ago. If she got one more phone call from her mom asking questions about how to use her cell phone, she'd scream.

CHAPTER THREE

WORKING THE PHONES

CAMERON connected her phone to the Bluetooth in her Jeep, and she cruised down the Long Island Expressway.

"Call Casey." Casey Keane was the head of NE tech support for SmartTech and one of Cameron's favorite people. He was the stereotypical nerd whose love for Mountain Dew was legendary. And he took off work every time a new Star Wars movie got released.

"Thanks for calling SmartTech, this is Casey."

"Casey, it's Cameron."

"Dude, you do know it's three thirty on a Friday."

"You say that like I can't just be calling to chat, like I only call you when there's a problem," she teased, trying to lighten his mood before making the request she knew he'd hate.

"Really?" he replied, not buying it for a minute. "You just called to say hi?"

"I just left Barry Issacs' place."

"Oh great." Casey knew Barry almost as well as she did, even though he never left the office. He had a reputation as a frequent and troublesome tech support caller. And never a particularly nice one. "Can't you tell me on Monday?"

"He's got problems with HomeTech Hubs."

"Him and everyone else on the planet. Why don't people realize these things aren't magic? They don't just do things without having proper hardware and programming in place. They can't turn on the lights if they don't have smart lighting! They aren't psychic, and they aren't real humans. Why can't people just ask them for the weather and be happy?"

Cameron smiled to herself, agreeing. It was a rant she'd heard from him many times before. She had to always be careful to not get him started on the misnomer about the name of the hubs. He could go on for hours about AI not being real and the evils of marketing in the tech industry.

"Your mouth to God's ears, but look, he's got a problem with the hubs integrating with a large system. He gave me two. Both units of the same lot, sequential serial numbers. One works, one doesn't. He wants us to test them in the R & D lab and see what the deal is.

"We're not going to test third-party products."

"C'mon, aren't you curious too? Haven't you gotten zillions of support calls on these things? Wouldn't it be nice to finally have a definitive answer to what their problem is? We have two perfect test units right here. You know you can't resist."

"Yes, I can. You're just going to have to break it to Barry. For support on those things, he must call Synergistic. We won't touch them."

"Fucking asshole," Cameron shouted as a car cut in front of her, leaving the carpool lane with no warning.

"Seriously?" Casey said hesitantly.

"Not you. Some jackass just decided to leave the carpool lane at a double line and almost clipped me. Standard New York driving. I hate this city."

"You love it."

"I know, but some days…. Anyway, is that your final answer? I'll buy you a case of Mountain Dew?"

"Final answer, but I'll take the Dew anyway for all the crap I put up with for you already. I spent two hours this week on the phone with one of your accounts walking him through troubleshooting shades. *Shades*! They go up. They go down. It's the easiest thing to install, and he couldn't get it right. You owe me a case for that just on principle." Casey sighed on the other end of the line. "Look, Cameron, I know it sucks, but it's a Pandora's box. If we look at one of those things, we'd have to look at them all. You'll think of something to tell Barry, but unfortunately, we just can't do it."

Well, shit. On the plus side, when she called Barry with the bad news on Monday, at least she could just hang up the phone. Or even better, she could just send an email.

CHAPTER FOUR

THERAPY

"ANYBODY on yet?" Cameron asked after logging into her weekly Friday conference call via the Bluetooth in her car.

Cameron's Friday call tended to be the highlight of her week. There were occasions where she had a great lunch or dinner with clients that trumped it, but those instances were becoming rare, or maybe she was just getting cynical. When she joined the SmartTech team, she was intimidated. Luckily, she ended up working with who she affectionately called the wonder twins: Bill and Phil. There were a lot of jokes when she joined the team that they should call her Jill. She squashed that idea pretty quickly. She didn't even like her own name abbreviated, much less a ridiculous rhyming nickname. She was Cam or Cameron, and that was it. Not

Cami, Cammy, or any other deviation.

The guys couldn't be more different, but they were the best teammates and friends she'd ever had. Together the three of them made up the Northeast Residential Sales team. They were always at the top of the leaderboard for sales company wide and had come to lean heavily on each other to make it happen consistently.

"I'm here," said Bill. He was the New England guy, and she called him her surrogate big brother. He was also the most technical of all of them. They weren't allowed to sit next to each other at any sales meetings anymore because of their shenanigans.

"You sound like shit," she answered, noting his deep voice. A sure sign he'd been out drinking the night before. A common occurrence more and more frequently since he'd begun dating again after his divorce.

"Yeah, I went out with Lacey again last night." He sighed wearily. "She's a lot of work."

"I'm driving, so I don't have my spreadsheet out. Which one is she?"

When Bill began dating after his divorce, he'd done so with gusto. He'd signed up for every dating app on the market. He had more dates in a week than Cameron had all year. She tried to support him, but between all the one-and-dones and girls he'd seen a few times, she started to lose track of who was who. The situation reached critical mass when she realized he was simultaneously dating three Emilys and he hadn't even realized it. So, she did what any good sales rep would do: she created an online spreadsheet for tracking and collaborative purposes. This way she could reference it when he talked about his dates to save him from recapping info she already knew, and it saved him from contacting the wrong girls or using the wrong names.

"She's the one who worked for a dealer who I hit the casinos with," he replied. "I think I'm done with her. I'm not as young as I used to be."

"Eh, heard that before," she replied.

"I'm winning this week. Boy, do I have a good one!" Phil broke in, saving her from having yet another conversation about Bill's out-of-control sex life. Phil split the NYC area with her, and she called him her crazy uncle. He was the hardest-working guy she knew, and he also had the biggest heart.

"Doubt it," she said. "I just left Barry Issacs."

The answering groans made her chuckle. It seemed like she'd told enough Barry stories that they knew how painful he could be. Learning from her team and leaning on them through the stressful time when she first started was what made her job the most enjoyable she'd ever had.

Somewhere after her second year with the company, and after she'd nursed them both through messy divorces, they began implementing this weekly call. It was kept private, and they only ever discussed one thing: who had had the most painful week. And they never ever talked about their quotas. It was a numbers-free zone.

They each got to pitch one story, and then they declared a winner. It served to lighten the mood and lead them all into the weekend in a positive way. In their business, it was hard to do, and they all discovered it was vital to their success.

"It's my turn first," Bill interjected. "I won last week."

"Go ahead, man," Phil said.

Cameron put her phone on mute so she could listen to the story and not distract them with any spontaneous outbursts at bad drivers.

"Okay, I saw Francois this week, and you guys know he's building that new school and training facility to educate more people in our industry. He wants SmartTech to give him for free, mind you, one of everything we make. He's been a dealer for almost fifteen years. He knows we don't give anything away free. So when I tell him this, and not for the first time, he completely trips out. He starts cursing at me, and after a while, he switches over to French, and I don't even think he noticed. So after a good five minutes of what I can only assume is him cursing me in a foreign language, I interrupt him to remind him that I don't speak French. He just stared at me for a minute, said, 'You got the point,' and then kicked me out of his office."

She unmuted herself so she could join in Phil's laughter. She felt her stress fade just a bit. Sharing their war stories was a great idea. Sales was a largely thankless job; no one ever called unless they had a problem or needed a favor. It helped knowing she wasn't the only one who put up with crazy for a living. Sometimes her job felt less like sales and more like babysitting or herding cats.

"That was a good one." Phil chuckled. "But I've still got you beat. I got a call from an end user yesterday saying her shades didn't work with the SmartTech app. So, I ask her who her dealer was. She has no idea. I ask if there's a way to find out. She gets frustrated and says she paid a hundred dollars for this app, and it should just work. So, I'm trying to talk her down and get any info from her so I can find her dealer. I ask for any serial numbers from any of her equipment so I can look up her dealer. She says she doesn't have any equipment."

"Man, this isn't a winner," said Bill. "I've had this conversation with tons of end users. They never know where their gear is."

"No, here's the best part. After thirty minutes, I discover she doesn't have SmartTech shades. In fact, she doesn't have motorized shades at all. She just has whatever blinds came with the place when she moved in. She thought the app would magically transform them into motorized shades somehow."

"Oh my God, that's fantastic," Cameron exclaimed. "Unbelievable. I don't even need to go. You win. That's a classic."

"No kidding. I won't even get into how pissed she got when I told her I couldn't credit her money back for the app and she had to reach out to Apple," Phil said.

"Agreed. Phil's the winner for the week. We all owe you a drink," Bill said, adding to the imaginary drink tally that they'd never use. Thank God for business expense accounts. "Even though it's moot, what was your story going to be, Cameron?"

"Well, it pales in comparison now, but I was going to tell you how Barry wore me down and got me to agree to commit to taking two HomeTech Hubs to R & D for testing and Casey shot me down. We won't touch them."

"Yikes," Phil put in. "So what are you going to do?"

"I'll figure something out. But not until Monday." That got chuckles out of both of them. "Listen, not to cut this short, but I just got into the tunnel. I'm going to be pulling into my garage soon, and the Maker's is calling my name, so I'll let you guys go. Thank you both for those stories. Always a good start to the weekend. I'll chat with you guys on the Monday morning call."

"Look at you not having to work on a weekend," replied Phil. "I've still got to finish my weekly report for the boss man."

"Freakin' Steve," Cameron said.

"Freakin' Steve," Bill agreed.

With that rejoinder on their boss, they all signed off as she navigated through the crowded Manhattan streets. Just like her job, driving in the city had been intimidating at first, but now it was second nature. She smiled to herself amidst the horns and the noise of the traffic. All things considered, she was a very lucky girl.

CHAPTER FIVE

YOU CAN TAKE THE GIRL OUT OF KENTUCKY

AFTER arriving back at her apartment a little before six and dropping her bags on the floor, the first thing Cameron did was put on her sweatpants and take off her bra. The second thing she did was pour herself a bourbon. Traffic wasn't that bad, but she sat for at least an hour after getting through the tunnel. Usually, reverse commuting saved her time, but you could never really foresee traffic patterns in Manhattan.

Her apartment was small, only five hundred square feet, but she prided herself on making it feel spacious. Storage containers and levels had become a necessity in a way she never could've imagined before moving to the city. Plopping on her bright red couch, the only pop of color in a predominantly monochromatic decorating scheme, she cracked her laptop open and took the first sip of her drink. Perfect. Now she could relax, clear out her inbox, and then, fingers crossed, have a work-free weekend.

Cameron had taken a lot of grief from her parents over the years for not being married. It wasn't that she was anti-marriage, per se. Her parents had been married for over forty years before her father passed. If she was being honest, she knew she just couldn't see herself committing to anything for that long. She almost had an anxiety attack buying her apartment, and she could sell that if she changed her mind. Traditionally, Cameron had a two-year cap on relationships, and that seemed to be working out well for her. She probably worked too much, but it was tough getting ahead in a male-dominated field, and to be taken seriously, she had to work twice as hard as her male counterparts. Realistically, Cameron knew it wasn't her job that kept her single. She liked coming home on a Friday night at the start of a weekend and not worrying about what someone else might have planned, or want for dinner, or that they may want to talk. Her whole job was talking, and at the end of a long day, the lack of having to interact with anybody seemed like bliss.

"AIME, play U2."

Cameron had plugged in the HomeTech Hubs when she finished responding to her last email. She was also on her second cocktail and had a firm rule not to send anything work related in writing after two drinks. It never turned out well.

As music filled the apartment, she smiled. It seemed

like that hub worked okay. Voice command seemed to be working. As she listened to "Where the Streets Have No Name," she plugged in the other hub, the one Barry claimed was defective.

After pairing the device and doing some basic setup, she played a round of twenty questions with AIME. The hub won. The hub always won, and it frustrated Cameron to no end. She was a competitive person, as most salespeople were, and losing to a machine didn't sit well.

She was in sales, not a technical person or a programmer, and that meant her troubleshooting skills were limited, so she walked herself through the basics steps she knew.

Pulling up the app on her phone, she checked for available updates. Nada. She opened the settings menu and checked the firmware. All up to date, and both devices were running the same version. No issue there. Of course it couldn't be that easy.

She pulled her spare box of hardware and demo units out from under her bed and began sorting through them. Since it was a network-based product, she'd tried both units with different routers and wireless access points. The long, painstaking process of configuring wireless networks took up the better part of her next hour and the rest of her second drink. They worked fine on whatever combination she tried.

With that, she was out of ideas and was beginning to wonder if there was really something wrong with one of the HomeTech Hubs or if it was simply a case of user error. It happened more frequently than any of her customers wanted to admit. They'd call her furious that a component she sold had arrived defective. They'd scream and complain, and when the factory received the piece back and tested it, they found nothing wrong. Once they'd received the replacement part, they'd have the same issue, and once her tech team walked them through the installation, the units would work, and the dealer would have egg on their face. But they never admitted it was their error; pride was rampant in her line of work. SmartTech estimated about thirty percent of all their returns came back as no problem found. It was a vicious cycle with Cameron stuck in the middle playing referee between the engineers and their customers so no one got their feelings hurt and business could continue as usual. It could be exhausting.

With her technical expertise tapped out and her team unwilling to get involved, Cameron was satisfied that she'd done all she could for Barry. In conclusion, it was a software issue in the HTH. Synergistic needed to write some new code. Probably new drivers. She'd write him a report tomorrow after her yoga class and offer him some credit on his account for his trouble. In her business, most problems were solved by throwing money at it. As long as Barry thought he won, they could move forward, and he'd continue to be one of her biggest accounts. At the end of the day, the dollars toward her quota were all that mattered.

She disconnected both devices and left them on the hardwood floor of her apartment. She'd box them back up in the morning. A movie had just come out in the theater she'd wanted to watch, so she pulled a Raspberry PI out of her messenger bag and plugged it into her TV. It was a gift from a satisfied customer. The small computer had software on it to stream any movie or TV show so long as another user was sharing it. Legal? Maybe not so much, but it was an awesome thank-you gift, and Cameron was going to take advantage. It sure beat paying for cable.

After the movie was over, Cameron planned to go to bed. She had yoga early in the morning, and getting up on a Saturday was always hard for her. But that yoga class was the only hour the whole week when she unplugged and turned off all her devices, and she desperately needed it for her mental health.

She had planned to leave it alone hours ago, but two more drinks had made her curious about the hubs again, and as she tripped over them on the way to her bedroom, she decided to give it one last go.

Cameron walked to the hall closet and dug into the back for an old toolbox a long-ago boyfriend had left behind. She dragged the heavy box out, wiped the dust off the top, and reached inside for a screwdriver. If the software wasn't the issue, maybe something in the hardware was defective. She'd just take both units apart and have a look.

If she weren't four cocktails into the evening, she'd have realized the futility of that idea. She had no way to test any of the individual components that make up the HTH, much less the know-how to even approach something like that. Her brain was pretty foggy, and when she plopped down on the floor with the screwdriver in her hand, she'd passed the point of analytical thought. So, like the layman she was, she tore into the HomeTech Hubs and began taking them apart.

CHAPTER SIX

MORNINGS ARE A BITCH

THE shrill beeping of her cell phone alarm jolted Cameron awake with a vengeance on Saturday morning. She reached over with a groan and turned it off. It was so tempting to sink back into the haze embellished by her white-noise machine. But if she did that, then she'd miss her yoga class and feel like a slug all weekend. Plus, she needed to hit the market on her way back. Her cupboards were chronically bare due to her long hours and dinners out wining and dining her customers. She was going to be home all weekend. No reason not to cook, although it was tempting to order in every night since everything in New York could be delivered. But she got her fill of eating out during the week with her clients. This was her time.

If she forced herself to get up now, she could get all

her errands done early and spend her afternoon watching football. If she was really lucky, Kentucky might even pull off a win.

She pushed herself up and staggered into the kitchen. She grabbed her standard breakfast of Diet Coke and chugged it with two Advil. It was her usual hangover cure, and that combined with a shower should have her moving at normal speed in no time. Stripping off her clothes and getting into the shower felt more challenging than usual, probably due to the bourbon. After she was out and dressed in her workout clothes, she was beginning to feel like a human being again. She'd headed out of the bathroom, blindly walking through her living room to the opposite side to hit the switch for her automated shades. She really should take the time to sync them with her HTH so she could raise them with voice commands, but somehow, she just never got around to it. It felt too much like work for her to play with tech on her off time.

Blackout shades in NYC were a godsend. With all the light pollution in the city, it was hard to sleep without them. But they really did black out all the light, and in her haze, she hadn't flipped the light switch, so she just had very little ambient light from her hallway to guide her. It wasn't enough, she realized, as she stepped on a sharp piece of plastic lying on her floor. She jumped up, grabbing her foot in pain, and as she landed, her other foot smashed down on something else sharp and she shrieked, windmilled her arms as she lost her balance, and promptly fell on her ass. In her shock, Cameron burst out laughing, thankful no one was there to see that display of grace. But what had she stepped on? She wasn't a clean freak by any stretch of the imagination, but she generally kept her floors clean. She had to; she had a remote vacuum cleaner she scheduled to sweep her place while she was working, and it wouldn't be good to get it caught on something when she wasn't home. Theoretically, it was supposed to turn itself off if it jammed, but being in the industry had taught her that what machines were supposed to do and what they actually did wasn't always the same thing.

Cameron reached out and grabbed the offending object, picking it up to examine it.

Oh yeah, she remembered now. She took apart Barry's HomeTech Hubs last night. She hoped she could put them back together, or better yet, maybe Barry wasn't expecting them back. Worst-case, she'd just buy him two new ones if they were beyond her ability to fix. They were cheap. She could eat that as payment for her drunken act of stupidity. Maybe it would help her learn her lesson, and next time she felt the urge to get creative, she'd just go to bed.

It was there, sitting in the pitch black of her apartment, throbbing pain in both feet, hair wet from the shower, that Cameron made the discovery that would change the course of her life. Giving her foot a final rub, she swept the pieces of the HomeTech Hubs away from where she was sitting, clearing herself space to get up without any additional incidents. Pushing the last piece aside, she stopped. Something caught her eye. There was a faint glow coming from one of the pieces. *Impossible*, she thought. Both units were trashed and incapable of working. They were also unplugged and had no batteries or internal power source. There shouldn't be any way anything could be glowing on that device; it must have been a reflection.

It was faint, and there was no way she would've noticed it with any light on, probably the reason she hadn't noticed it the night before in her fervor of deconstruction and bourbon. But there it was. A soft green light coming from one of the pieces. Even in pitch black, the light was barely visible, and she had to focus to see it, but there was no doubt. Something on this device was getting power from something. But why? And how? It was a cheap consumer product. It didn't cost enough to have any of the advanced technology that would keep something powered without a source. Sure, there were things available to do that, but they were expensive. Much too expensive to add to a cheap device. And certainly not necessary on a product that lived indoors and would be able to be constantly plugged in.

With a sick feeling in her stomach that had nothing to do with the booze from last night, Cameron set the piece on her coffee table. She got up, turned the lights on, and raised the blackout shades. Slowly she made her way back to her couch and hesitantly picked up what she could now see was a computer board. The light wasn't visible now, but she could see the indicator it came from. It was a small part. Less than an inch square. Setting it back down on the coffee table, she moved again to the floor and started digging through the parts of both hubs that she had disassembled the prior evening. She missed her yoga class in her focus, but she kept searching. She busied herself playing a solo version of the strangest match game ever.

Finally, after an hour, she gave up. It wasn't there. There wasn't a duplicate to the piece that was on her table. She'd meticulously laid out every part of both hubs on her floor with its corresponding twin right next to it. All the pieces were there. Two complete units. She looked under the couch, in the kitchen, even in the bedroom, though she knew she wouldn't find it.

Cameron Caldwell had discovered why some HomeTech Hubs failed and others didn't. But it wasn't an answer at all.

She picked up the circuit board on her coffee table one more time and examined it. She knew enough to know it was a transmitter of some kind. She knew it had to be expensive since it could power itself. And she knew beyond a shadow of a doubt that whatever it did, it wasn't good, and it wasn't supposed to be there.

CHAPTER SEVEN

WHAT DO YOU MEAN, YOU DON'T HAVE AN IPHONE?

WILL wasn't having a good start to his Saturday. It was six in the morning, and he was standing, untouched coffee in his hand, in the misty rain in front of the Synergistic Engineering headquarters on 29th Street. Detective William Justus had been an NYPD homicide detective for seven years, and he was acutely aware of the irony of his last name. Some days it seemed like everyone he met commented on it. It was a credit to his laidback nature that it didn't even faze him anymore.

The one thing this crime scene had going for it so far was that it was on the same block as a great local coffee shop. He couldn't even begin to wrap his mind around what the eight-story former hotel had cost the company not only to purchase but to renovate. The interior was wasted, in his opinion, with too much open space. Space being such a commodity in the city, a native New Yorker like Will resented the opulence it represented. He lived in a small two-bedroom apartment in Greenpoint that he bought long before the neighborhood had become gentrified. That was the only reason he could afford to live there now. Prices in the city kept rising, driving working people farther and farther out to make room for the elite and the foreign investors who owned apartments they didn't even live in. It was good for him though. He planned to cash out on his retirement. Take his measly police pension and the profits from that apartment and buy himself a place in the country. Far away from the throngs of people and the worst of humanity. Cynical? Hell, maybe he was. But he'd dare anyone to point out any NYC cops with as many years on the force as he had who weren't.

The first floor of the Synergistic building was leased to several bespoke clothing companies he was sure he couldn't afford to buy a sock from. The lobby of the business was still as large as a storefront. All he could think was that it was a terribly vain waste to have such a showy entrance when the monthly rent for a business there would earn tens of thousands of dollars a month.

It wasn't that he hated tech people, or rich people in general. It was just that they had a way of looking down on him, either for his lack of technical know-how or his lack of finances. Will was a Luddite. He didn't have a smartphone. He only carried a mobile phone as a consequence of his job. He didn't participate in social media; he didn't stream anything. He didn't even have Wi-Fi at his apartment. They had it at the station, and that was enough for him. It was unusual for someone his age. His generation was the first to grow up with computers. Pagers and cell phones started to gain popularity when he was in high school. But unlike his peers, he didn't embrace the technology, and joining the Army lessened his exposure to it. By the time he opted out of his service and used the military to fund his education, he wasn't interested in catching up on the current trends. He knew enough to get by, but he preferred the outdoors to sitting in front of a computer; and for the life of him, he couldn't understand the appeal of scrolling through a feed of people he used to know trying to outdo each other and prove how great their lives were. He had to pretend his friends' kids were cute in person; he didn't need to do it online too.

Police detectives in New York weren't exactly raking in the big bucks. During a murder investigation, people's worst traits tended to come out, and the situation was always worse when dealing with the wealthy. Their lack of respect for his authority, their sense of entitlement, and their quick calls to their lawyers almost always impeded an investigation.

And that's why Detective William Justus was pissed off. Standing on the street, trying to inhale his coffee and waiting for his partner.

Will watched his partner, Detective Alan Jones, walk out of the doorway to Synergistic and give him a wave.

"What have we got?" he said, dispensing with the pleasantries, as was his custom, and getting right to the point.

"Cleaning crew found him," Alan replied in his slow, even way. Nothing seemed to rattle him. A twenty-two-year veteran of the force, he'd passed on retirement two years ago to increase his pension. He had two daughters and one granddaughter, and according to him, girls were expensive. But with his experience in the city, he'd pretty much seen it all. And in contrast to Will, he was the first person in their precinct to purchase any new technology that came on the market. "The victim is twenty-eight-year-old engineer Matteo Rodriguez. Matt to his friends. He's loaded. Practically a god in these circles. He's the one who invented the HTH."

"The what?"

"Really? The HomeTech Hub? Everyone has one of those. Got mine for the kids, They love it. Grandkid does too. Delia says she doesn't, but I catch her talking to it sometimes."

Will was nodding along, half paying attention, until he heard the last part. "What? Talking to it?"

"Yeah, it's an artificial intelligence device. You say anything starting with 'AIME,' you know, like AI for Me, but pronounced like the girl's name, Amy. Anyway, it'll give you an answer. You can ask about the weather, sports scores, make a phone call, ask how many cups are in a gallon, whatever, and it answers you."

"I don't get it."

"I don't expect you would, but it's the hottest thing out right now. You can use it to listen to music, shop from it, and a million other things. The best part is that it hooks into the thermostat and learns what you like. That way Delia and the girls can't overdo it on the air-conditioning and freeze me out when I get home. Not to mention it saves me a pretty penny too."

"You can't be serious."

"Oh sure, and that's not all. Companies are going nuts trying to tie into this thing and monetize it. It's already made this company over a billion dollars."

"Now *that* I understand," Will said, finishing his coffee and throwing it in the nearby trash can before reaching for the door handle. "And that's worth killing over.

Their conversation continued as they entered the building and nodded at the receptionist, who was desperately trying to stop crying and pull it together. They continued to the elevator. Will stopped and stared at the wall next to the door. There were no buttons. It had a black scanner-like pad instead. Sort of like what was on a grocery checkout. He stared at it for a beat, then slowly ran his hand back and forth in front of it, trying to figure it out. The chuckle from his right told him he was getting it very wrong.

Alan held his phone up to the scanner, and the doors closed and began to take them up to the eighth floor.

"We've got to get you a smartphone, man. What would you've done if I hadn't been here?"

With a slow grin creeping on his face, showing the dimples that made him look younger than his forty-one years, he replied, "Stairs, man. I would've taken the stairs."

"Victim Matteo Rodriguez, chief engineering officer at SE. He earned a scholarship to MIT, where he majored in computer science and engineering, then on to a master's in mechanical engineering. Fit guy, he was a rock climber. Cause of death was blunt force trauma to the head," Alan recited. "He was beaten repeatedly with a crowbar. Found it at the scene. Looks like the victim stayed late at the office last night, which, according to everyone asked, is not unusual. Was working at his computer when someone snuck up behind him and hit him several times in the head. We'll know more once the ME takes a look, but that's the gist."

"Any sign of a break-in?"

"Nope, not a thing," he replied, closing the notebook app on his phone that he had been reading from. "And let me tell you something else. It isn't easy to get in this place. At night or otherwise. There's a security guard. Keycards are required to enter all doors and the stairwells, including the one to the victim's office he was killed in. You saw the elevator. It identifies everyone who uses it by their phone."

"Don't they have security cameras in a place like this? Seems we should at least be able to take advantage of all the technology in here."

"Disabled."

Will swore under his breath. *Figures.*

"What about the keycard access? Does it show whose was used?

"It was the victim's. Our tech guys say at a place like this, that means nothing. It could've been cloned, hacked to make it look that way, or any number of options. If whoever did this was smart enough to get past the cameras, the rest of it was just easy."

Will sighed. Not good news.

The elevator dinged. They finally reached the crime scene.

"You know, Al, I think I'm really going to hate this case."

CHAPTER EIGHT

SATURDAY, WAIT. BUT SUNDAY ALWAYS
COMES TOO LATE.

CAMERON Caldwell hadn't moved in some time. After making her discovery that morning, she'd dropped the shades back down, turned the lights off, and stared at the glowing green dot on her coffee table. Just to convince herself she wasn't losing her mind. She'd stood up and paced for a bit, but mostly she just sat there, in the dark, staring as she tried to figure out what to do next.

Her brain was racing with the possibilities of what the device could be used for when it hit her. That was the wrong question. The better question was what *couldn't* it be used for? This thing was implanted in the HTH, which was connected to and given a password to the user's home network. It could get into and gather information from any device connected to the home network. And with the right programming, it could get anything. It could get the date, time, and location information. See when your TVs were on, what you were watching. It could access your surveillance cameras, download videos of you in your house when you thought no one was watching. If whoever did this was clever enough—and at this point, she had to assume they were—they could even get into all the computers brought into the home. Download any information the user had. Because they were given access when you connected the hub. Anyone bringing a laptop home from the office with corporate secrets or people's stored photos and videos. All of it could be gathered with something like this.

But how did it work? How often did it transmit? If it could discern location information, would someone know where the device was now? Could they realize it had been tampered with? Her mind was spinning with the possibilities.

Her stomach growled, bringing her back to reality and making her realize it was almost lunch and she hadn't eaten anything all day besides her Diet Coke and Advil. Breakfast of champions. And really, if she stepped back from it a little, it probably wasn't that bad. This may be the only hub affected. It could be a bug planted by a PI or something. She didn't know anything about the guy whose house this came from. He could be going through a messy divorce, and his wife could be spying on him. Or he could be a criminal, and this device could've been planted by the government. Or the cops. There could be any number of reasonable explanations for it that didn't have anything to do with a crazy conspiracy or anything like that. She'd been watching way too many spy movies.

Regardless, it was Saturday. Her office was closed until Monday, so even if she wanted to, there wasn't anything she could do about it now.

Once she decided to put it out of her mind, she did her best to forget everything HTH related and get on with her day. Shaking out of the mental wormhole she'd sucked herself into, she went back to the original plan for her day. She took a later yoga class and hit the farmers market after. She still had flashes of thought about the endless nefarious possibilities of that extra chip, but doing her best to put it behind her, she made herself a nice dinner and went to bed early.

Relaxed and less worried about the chip in her living room, Cameron woke up on Sunday feeling refreshed and ready for football. It was NFL day, and the Giants actually had a team this year. She threw on her jeans, an Eli hoodie, and stepped into her flats that she'd left by the door. Pulling her long brown hair up into a ponytail, and not interested in taking the time to put in her contacts, she grabbed her glasses and headed to the bodega downstairs.

They made a killer breakfast sandwich, and the coffee was pretty good too. In the five years she'd lived in her building, she had become a regular fixture.

"Hey, Eytan," she called in greeting to the owner as she walked in the door to the little shop.

"The usual?" he asked, ignoring the line of customers in front of the counter. It paid to be a regular sometimes.

Her usual was a bacon and egg sandwich and vanilla latte.

"You bet," she replied. It was nice to be known here. Feel a sense of community in a big city she was still learning, even after half a decade of residency. She'd never regretted moving to New York, but it was hard at first not knowing anyone. Having the guy at the bodega know your name and what you liked was a small thing, but it went a long way into making her feel like she belonged.

Cameron browsed the shop while she waited for her sandwich and coffee to be made. She needed to replenish some spices if she was going to make her famous chili that day. It was mid-November, and the weather was finally cold enough to make the first chili of the season.

Making chili on Sunday during the NFL games always made Cameron think of her father. It was his secret recipe she used. Now that he had passed away, it was shared only with her brother and her. Rush Caldwell was an accomplished attorney in his day. Cameron remembered that growing up, she thought her father was the smartest man in the world. He finished the *New York Times* Sunday crossword puzzles, and he did it in pen. He knew all the answers on *Jeopardy!* and he read books constantly. Those memories made his disease even worse. Rush had suffered from dementia in the last years of his life, and the memory loss and confusion were hard for him to take. It was hard for the whole family. The regression she saw her father take was rapid. Drastically changing his personality what felt like overnight. But he would like this though, she thought. He was always proud of his chili, entering it in local chili cookoffs and mostly winning. He'd like that she still made it when the weather turned cool, and that it reminded her of him.

Smiling to herself and happy with her memories, Cameron realized she hadn't thought about the dismantled HTH in her apartment since she left there. As she walked to the counter to pay for and collect her breakfast, she grabbed a copy of the *Post*, then prepared to snag one of the five stools the bodega kept in the window to eat and watch the world go by on a Sunday morning. That was until she saw the headline on the front page of the *Post*.

Twenty-eight-year-old genius and HomeTech Hub inventor Matteo Rodriguez found murdered in Synergistic office Saturday morning; police have no leads.

Then she froze and knew no matter what she tried to tell herself, something was very wrong with the HomeTech Hubs.

CHAPTER NINE

EVERYBODY'S WORKING WEEKENDS

SUNDAY brought nothing but pain for Will and his partner. Stuck in the conference room at the 10th precinct waiting on his boss, Will was not pleased to be there. Saturday had been a long day for them at the SE offices. After the discovery of the body, the ME and crime scene investigators descended to do their work while Will and Alan interviewed the member of the cleaning staff who discovered the body. She was a sixty-two-year-old woman who was traumatized and seemed to know nothing of consequence to their investigation. There were a few staff members on hand they spoke to, none who had been there last Friday night or entered the victim's office. All did seem to agree on one thing: they needed to speak to Trey, aka Wilson Howell III and the owner of the company. Barring that, they needed either Trey's best friend and firm attorney, Brandon Reece, or the VP of sales, Tessa Wells.

With a small bit of detecting work, they discovered all the officers and most of the staff were at a party in the Hamptons that weekend. They were at a company celebration for the sale of the ten millionth HomeTech Hub. Which only begged the question as to why the inventor wasn't there himself?

Luckily, Will didn't have to make the notification to the next of kin. Since the victim's family was from Texas, they'd worked with a local police officer to handle the notification there. Both parents would be flying to New York the following day, and Will and Alan would meet with them then. Never a pleasant part of the job.

Captain Gil Lovett barged into the conference room in his usual loud manner. Everything about the thirty-year NYPD veteran was loud. His talk, his manners, and his attitude. He was an old-school kind of cop who didn't believe in a lot of bullshit, either giving or receiving, and Will liked that about him. He appreciated that Captain Lovett didn't kowtow to the politicians the way some others did. It meant he'd never again move up in rank. But Will didn't suppose that mattered much to Gil. He was more interested in catching criminals. A tall, attractive man in his sixties, Gil Lovett was still a ladies' man, never having settled down. He claimed to be too married to his job. It was possible, when looking at his captain, that Will was seeing himself in twenty years.

Lovett slammed a copy of the *New York Post* on the table with authority and simply stated, "This one is going to be a real mess, boys. What've you got?"

"The ME placed the time of death somewhere between seven and midnight Friday night. We'll know more after the autopsy. The medical examiner agreed to come in today to do it. We're meeting him down there at noon." Alan began laying out what they'd learned for the captain. He rose out of his chair and stood in front of the large dry erase board they'd begun compiling information on, gesturing to it as he went. "Initial report, blunt force trauma to the head. The weapon was a crowbar, no prints, no unique identifiers. There was construction on the second floor of the building. The weapon probably came from there, so no leads."

"Discovered by a member of the cleaning crew the following morning," Will chimed in, wanting to be useful before they reached the technical part he didn't understand. "No help, didn't see anything, didn't hear anything. Wasn't in the office the previous evening. We'll run the standard checks, but she wasn't involved."

"So, what do you know?"

"Unfortunately, not much," Will replied. "What we have now is a lot of questions. First, why was the victim in his office? Most everyone else from the company was at the owner's house in the Hamptons for a company party. Why wasn't such an integral member of the team there? And why didn't anyone notice his absence? We've been unable to communicate with any of the employees from SE due to their travel, but they'll all be back in the city tomorrow, and we have interviews with the top three executives with their attorneys. We'll see where that takes us before we start interviewing the other employees. At last count, SE employed over 500 people, though most of them in overseas factories. Only about 150 at the New York office. Alan will have to tell you about the technical part."

"Lawyered up already, huh?" Captain Lovett commented, annoyed at having hoops to jump through this early in the investigation.

"Whoever did this was very tech savvy. They disabled all the cameras in the building. Which, with what SE does and what I could glean looking at their system, is very advanced. We'll know more tomorrow when we speak to them, but this wasn't your average burglar. They also reformatted his computer, deleting everything on it. Did the same to his phone, destroyed his cloud account, and broke into the server room and stole some of the hard drives stored there. If I had to guess, it's likely we'll discover those were the victim's backup drives. We'll wait and see. But he didn't stop there. It looks like all the other drives were attacked. Most likely with a degausser."

"A what?" the captain asked, rubbing the space between his eyes. This case was already starting to get complicated.

"It's like a magnet you can use for destroying data. It's not 100 percent successful in a situation like this where most likely the plates will have something to protect them from magnetic attacks. However, some damage was done, though a lot will be recoverable with a lot of time and expense. We can offer to help SE with this if they let us near the drives, which they probably won't, but I think it's a waste of time. The killer was looking for and trying to get rid of something of the victim's. The attack on the other servers was just a secondary action. A smokescreen, if you will. He got rid of all the victim's data. That's all that mattered to him. Whether he took it with him or destroyed it all, we don't know.

"Basically, to sum it all up for you, Captain, a very technically oriented person went to a lot of trouble to kill Matt Rodriguez and get rid of all his data. What the killer was looking for, we don't know. We don't know who saw him last, we don't know if he was troubled or working on anything new. And the only people who can tell us are all also very technically adept people who've already lawyered up. Primarily the owner, one William Howell III, aka Trey, who's something of an enigma in the tech industry. A Massachusetts blue blood who chose to shun the family business of banking and enter the world of technology. Undoubtedly a genius. His success at Synergistic was in no small part to his family's influence. His grandfather, William the first, was a Massachusetts senator. His father, Will Two, was a banking titan. And even though his family cut him off financially when he chose to go his own path, the name still opened doors for Trey. So yeah, this one is going to be messy."

The captain rose from the chair where he'd been sitting, staring at the murder board and listening. He stood there for a minute with his head down toward the table before he looked up at them and spoke.

"You don't know much," he commented. "Before you head to the autopsy, reach out to the ADA. I know you guys can handle yourselves, but with the types of attorneys these guys have, it wouldn't be a bad idea to have a chat before you head over there tomorrow. Just to get an idea of what you'll be able to get a warrant for, etc. Mind your p's and q's on this one, boys. I've already received a call from One Police Plaza, and it's still the weekend. This thing is going to blow up tomorrow, so let's get all our ducks in a row and do this one by the book. I want updates twice a day. Do your best to close this one fast."

With that, the captain slammed out the door, and Will sighed. He met eyes with his partner across the ancient conference table and did something he swore he'd never do again. He called the cell phone of Kim Goodrich, the acting ADA, as instructed by the captain.

Kim was a very smart, driven, and beautiful woman... and an ex-girlfriend of Will's. Kim was a prep-school-taught Yale grad who was slumming it in the DA's office as so many do before making a run at a political career. She had it in her head that marrying a middle-class policeman would give her some street cred. Will didn't agree, and the breakup was volatile. The relationship was three years over, and Kim was now married to some hedge-fund guy, but that didn't stop her from making his life miserable every chance she could get.

Alan smirked at him as the phone rang. He'd never liked Kim and had tried to warn Will away many times during their relationship. He never verbally said, "I told you so," but those looks told a different story.

Will also wanted to dig into the lives of the three principals of SE. It was always good to be prepared for situations like this, and he had a feeling he'd need to be on his best game tomorrow. Not only in dealing with Kim but with their top three suspects as well.

CHAPTER TEN

LONE MEANS ONE

IT took everything Cameron had to be patient and wait until 9:00 a.m. Monday to go to the SmartTech offices. She did her Monday morning conference call with all the other SmartTech reps and her boss on mute, only half paying attention on her drive to the office. Her nerves finally started receding as she turned onto SmartTech Drive and began passing all the buildings her company owned. SmartTechs main facility was a gleaming monolith of glass and metal shining at the end of the drive. But to get there you had to pass all the R&D, production, shipping, and warehousing facilities. Fifteen massive buildings lining the street stretching for miles so by the time you reached the main office you were already suitably impressed with the grandeur of the company. The effect was a useful tool and she'd seen it work on customers. Their awe growing as they rode down the drive and were confronted with the reality of just how massive SmartTech was and that's just the way Steve designed it.

To say she was freaked out would be an understatement. After her discovery Sunday morning, she sat on the couch, TV on, football games and chili forgotten, and tried to come up with a plan. First, she had to know what the transmitter did. She couldn't do anything based on supposition. That's why she was at the office first thing on a Monday. Which anyone who knew her would know was an anomaly for her. For one thing, she worked remotely, visiting dealers in the field, and hardly went to her office at all, unless her day included giving end users a tour of the showroom on-site to close a sale. Mondays were also the day of the weekly team sales call. Eight o'clock sharp every Monday morning, the whole crew from every division logged on to get reamed out by their boss. No matter what their numbers were. On days she didn't have meetings, she worked from her home office, preferring it to sitting in traffic to drive to New Jersey where SmartTech was located and the distractions that came with an office setting. She was also not an early riser. Cameron was a night owl. If she had a choice, she'd rather stay up late and sleep for as long as she could.

On days like today, she'd sleep until seven forty-five before she'd roll out of bed, brush her teeth, and, without changing out of her pajamas, pop open her laptop and begin the day. But this Monday saw her up, showered, and in her Jeep by 6:30 a.m., ensuring no matter how bad traffic was, she'd get to the office so she could go in as soon as she was finished with her call, and Casey would already be there. She'd packed up the HomeTech Hubs, put on one of her best suits like she always did when any of her bosses might see her, and headed to New Jersey.

Barely stopping to greet Melissa, the receptionist, she hustled up the stairs of the main office to the second floor, which housed the tech support team. Rushing past the cubicles where the customer service team sat, she was relieved to see Casey in his office with his customary morning Mountain Dew. Casey Keane was a Stanford grad with little ambition and a mind for gadgets, which was what led him to SmartTech. After years of writing his own code and building computers, smart home integration was no challenge for him. Things Cameron could never comprehend were simple for Casey. And he liked his job of managing the tech support team. He only had to interact with his team and sales reps these days. He didn't take support calls anymore unless they were a particular challenge, which was best, as he was not the most patient or personable fellow. But Cameron liked him. She'd intentionally cultivated a good working relationship with him when she'd started so she'd have someone she could lean on in the support department. He'd also seemed to chill out a bit over the years, becoming especially more approachable in the last few months as he and his wife had welcomed their first baby. And although unambitious, he wasn't lazy, and he never let her down. She hoped today wouldn't be the first time.

She walked into his office holding the two HTH boxes,

setting them down on his desk, and not for the first time noticed the lack of any decoration in his little corner of the building. No pictures or tchotchkes to disrupt the space. Just an old-fashioned coffeepot. She'd offered to buy him a Keurig before when he'd helped her have a particularly good month, but he'd turned her down. She dropped her purse in one of the chairs that sat around the small table in front of his desk.

He looked up at her, and before even saying good morning, he said, "If those are for Barry Issacs, I told you we're not touching them." He sat back in his desk chair, crossing his arms over his chest, firm in his stance. "I'm not changing my mind."

Cameron put a finger to her mouth, motioning for him to stay quiet, then reached into her messenger bag, pulled out a single piece of paper, and handed it to him. She mouthed, "Read," while he looked at her quizzically.

"Let's go smoke a cigarette," she said, staring at him and shaking her head when he looked like he was beginning to speak. She gestured to the paper she'd handed him and made a show of reaching in her back pocket, grabbing her cell phone, and laying it on the desk. Then she slowly reached for her left arm and removed her fitness tracker, laying it on his desk as well. He stared at them for another few seconds before he finally looked at the note she'd handed him.

Don't say anything. Just remove any piece of technology you have on you, set it on your desk, and come outside with me.

She'd spent all day Sunday trying to come up with a plan

to figure out what the chip could do. She knew Casey could figure it out, but she didn't know how to explain it to him in front of the hub. If it was a transmitter, was it recording? Would it still transmit after she'd removed it from the Hub? Would it still wirelessly connect with the mic in the HTH and record anything she said? If it did, how could she tell him without it hearing her? And if it linked to other devices nearby, as it was designed to do, would her phone or fitness tracker relay information as well? She didn't want to overact and behave like a conspiracy nut, but the best way to be safe was to remove all her devices and get away from technology. The worst that could happen was he'd think she was crazy, and she could live with that.

Still looking at her strangely, he took both his cell phones and his smartwatch and set them on the desk. She reached into her purse to grab a pack of cigarettes and gestured to the door.

"I thought you quit," he asked as they headed out of his office and down the back stairs that would lead them to the smokers' area next to the employee parking lot.

"I started again yesterday." She'd been cigarette free for two years, but as soon as she'd seen the news in the paper yesterday morning, she'd grabbed a pack from the bodega and started again. It was a disgusting habit, and she hated herself a little for being so weak.

Reaching the metal picnic table outside in a small grass area reserved for smokers, Cameron lit a cigarette and began pacing.

"What the hell, Cameron?"

"Okay," she said as she continued to pace. "You're going to think I'm crazy, but I need your help. After I called you Friday, I went home, and I took Barry's HomeTech Hubs apart. And I found something. The unit he claims won't integrate has an extra board in it. It's a transmitter of some kind, and I need you to find out what it does."

"Okay, but what's with all the secrecy? You could've just told me in my office."

She reached into her inside jacket pocket, pulled out just the front page of Sunday's *New York Post*, and handed it to him.

"Wow, Matt Rodriguez is dead. That's crazy, but it still doesn't explain your level of paranoia."

"He was murdered, Casey, and I don't want to jump to conclusions, but what if it has something to do with that extra chip? The way I see it, there are two options here. One, it's an isolated thing. Some PI put it in there to catch a cheating spouse or something. No big deal, right? But what if it's not? How many calls do you get a day about these things not integrating into the system? What if the ones that don't work with SmartTech are all units with this extra piece in it, which means it's much more widespread?"

She stopped pacing and stubbed out her cigarette, then immediately lit another one before sitting down across from him at the table.

"I feel like those three nerds on *The X-Files*, but, Casey, these things have a lot of info in them. You could do some serious damage if you had an all-access pass to people's technology. Seriously, think about it for a second. What couldn't you do with this?

He sat for a minute, smoking and thinking before he replied.

"The Lone Gunmen."

"What?"

"From *The X-Files*, that's who you mean. The Lone Gunmen."

"No, there were three of them," she said slowly as if talking to a child.

"Yeah, The Lone Gunmen."

Frustrated she stood up and began pacing again. "Whatever. We've suddenly stumbled into the weirdest version of 'Who's on First' ever. Speculation is meaningless. Believe me, I've almost driven myself insane this weekend with what-ifs. We can't do anything until we know what it does. Can you find out? In the meantime, I'm going to reach out to Barry and find out who the customer is. I also need you to check a few of the HomeTech Hubs we have around here. We need to know if it's in more than one. Can you check some of the units dealers have sent us? Not ones sent by Synergistic, just to be sure?"

"I can do that. But, Cameron, pulling something like this off would be more complicated than you think. First, how would they get these chips in the units before they were sold? All the manufacturing would be done in an automated factory. You couldn't just add something to random units, someone would notice. And how could you manage where they were shipped to? If you were looking for dirt on people, it'd be a crapshoot. You'd have to hope one ended up somewhere useful."

"I thought about that, and I have two possible scenarios if this isn't an isolated incident. One, it was done after manufacturing at one location. Like a retail store or something. You could easily get a job at a big box store and slip the chips in after hours. Do it in a prominent enough zip code and the chances of getting sensitive information are pretty good. But we'll know that once you check a few units we have from across the country. If it's not, I have a theory. I spent a lot of time yesterday researching after my discovery, and right before Synergistic started production on the HTH, they opened a manufacturing facility in upstate New York. It was marketed as a way to bring jobs back to the US, and they got a ton of tax breaks for it. But what if only the units from that location have this chip in it? They manufacture a significantly lower number of hubs, so it would account for the percentage of failures being so small. And the cost to manufacture is higher because it's done in the States, so you could easily lose the extra cost of this device in there somewhere, and no one would know they were any different."

"Jesus, now I'm starting to believe you. And we could track the manufacturing locations by serial number if I find anymore chips."

"You know me, Casey. I'm not crazy."

"There's one thing you haven't thought of. If this is widespread and is in multiple homes across the country, what will this do to SmartTech? No one's going to want a home automation system if they can be hacked. Privacy concerns on our systems are already a big deal. It won't matter that the HomeTech Hubs aren't ours and our systems won't work with them. This will tank our business too. Are you going to tell Steve?"

Steve Perkins was the CEO of SmartTech, and everyone was terrified of him, including Cameron. Steve was a firm believer in leading by fear. Every member of the sales team knew all the unwritten rules. If you ever, for any reason, fell below 80 percent of quota, you got fired. Quarterly sales meetings were stressful exercises in abject humiliation for all of them when Steve publicly berated them one at a time. Calling them up to give a presentation on their region and nitpicking everything they said. Memories of her first presentation in front of Steve were still the stuff of nightmares; it was the closest Cameron ever came to crying at work. No member of the sales team ever voluntarily spoke to Steve. It was common practice to run the other way or duck into an open office if you saw him in the building. Cameron was one of two women on the sales team, and she especially went out of her way to avoid him. With a temper like she had, she sometimes feared her emotions would get the better of her, and she'd lose it in one of those meetings and go off on him. It hadn't happened yet, but every time they met, she worried about talking her way out of her job.

"Freaking Steve," she said. "I thought about that, and right now there's nothing to tell him. That's why we need to know if it's an isolated incident or not. It could be nothing. But if it is something, then you can tell him. He's nicer to the tech team."

Casey snorted and stubbed his cigarette out, knowing Cameron was trying to pass that landmine onto him. "Here's what we're going to do. We go back to my office. Talk normally about whatever in case this thing is listening. Show me the extra chip, and I'll test it. You go talk to Barry. I'll let you know when I find something."

CHAPTER ELEVEN

PROGRAMMERS ARE EASY

IT was two hours later before Cameron made it out to Barry's shop on Long Island. The traffic gods were with her today; on a bad day, it could've taken five. His office was back in an industrial complex midway between the city and the Hamptons, providing him with the perfect location to service both markets. Instead of feeling irritated that she was just here three days before, she was anxious, riding on the energy of finally delivering the unit to Casey and edging closer to getting some answers.

Her challenge would be getting Barry to tell her who the client was. He was a giant in his own mind and always tried to subtly allude to who his high-profile clients were without really saying it. Like every SmartTech customer wasn't "somebody." Their systems retailed for millions of dollars, but the shine of celebrity had worn off pretty soon after taking the job, and the mansions that once seemed like fairy tales were just houses to her these days. Hopefully this one wouldn't be a big thing, and he wouldn't be constricted by an NDA. But even if he were, there were other ways to find out. Traditionally his employees were less conspicuous than most. They'd never be so careless as to use the customer's name or address on POs or tech support calls as her less security conscious customers did. She only hoped she didn't have to dig that deep to get answers. Patience was not one of her virtues.

She parked her Jeep and took a deep breath. Reaching into the passenger seat, she grabbed the box of donuts she'd stopped for and headed inside the office.

Opening the front door, she rolled her eyes as she passed Barry's wall of infamy, barely glancing at her picture on the wall amongst the others. Getting past the assistant at the front door was easy. Barry's daughter was working the phones and the front desk in between getting her master's degree and her wedding, which seemed fast approaching. In no time, Cameron found herself in the back room sitting with two of Barry's techs.

Rob and Paul were working to build a rack when Cameron found them. Because it was filled with components, the delicate work of wiring the rack with different-colored wires in an intricate fashion was slightly mesmerizing to watch. Almost like weaving a very complex tapestry. Both were happy for the distraction and to talk and eat her donuts. Donuts were the secret weapon of salespeople, opening doors and getting purchase orders with every calorie. She'd started off casually, just shooting the shit, trying to find a subtle way to get the information she needed out of them. Over half an hour passed before she made her move.

"So Barry gave me some HomeTech Hubs on Friday. Were you guys on that job?"

"I was," Rob answered. "That Minsky project has been a shit show since the beginning. Those HomeTech Hubs were just the latest in a long line of issues."

Minsky. She had a last name.

"Oh yeah? That's a bummer," she replied, smiling to herself. "Is the homeowner being cool about it at least?"

"Mark? Yeah, he's an okay dude, and for the most part, his system has been functional. It's just a few little hiccups that have been persisting. The lighting keeps doing weird stuff. We'll get it straightened out soon enough."

Mark Minsky. Well, that was easier than I thought.

"Hey, just out of curiosity, are we your biggest dealer this year?"

Ah, vanity. Thy name is the AV guy. If she had a nickel for every time someone asked her that.

"I think you guys slipped down to third this year. But don't worry, you've still got a few months to catch up before the end of the year."

That ought to light a fire under them.

CHAPTER TWELVE

DISCOVERY

AN hour after pulling into Barry's shop, Cameron was back in her car and on her way to the Hamptons. Programmers were suckers. It took her forty-five minutes to get the information she needed from them and one google search to get the address. Turned out Mark Minsky had an article on his house written up in *Hamptons Magazine*, so she not only had the address, but she had pictures of the property as well. She was fortunate that Barry was out, or it might not have been so easy.

As she drove, Cameron engaged the Bluetooth in her Jeep and instructed the car to call Casey. He answered immediately and sounded stressed.

"What'd you find out?" she asked, bypassing the usual pleasantries as she took the exit off the LIE that would lead her to the Sunrise Highway and take her the rest of the way to the Hamptons.

"It's early, but I've got some preliminary info for you. Mostly because I've seen it before. First, you can let go of some of your paranoia. It can't record and transmit our conversations when the hub's unplugged, so we can speak freely around it. I'm still not sure if it picks up all connected data when it gets plugged back in, so we'll want to be careful about that. The chip is designed to aggregate all data from any connected device, then send all recorded information once a day. Looks like at midnight. It's nothing new. It's the same kind of chip everyone uses for keystroke trackers and parental safeguards."

"So basically, it's spyware," she stated, clarifying her understanding of what that meant. "Depending on the tech installed in a home, you'd have access to everything from all the data on any of their devices to when they come and go and what temperature they keep their thermostat set. It's a complete window into someone's life. Especially someone who has a SmartTech system. They'd have way more tech installed in their home than the average person."

"It's more than that. It syncs with all connected devices. That includes tablets, cell phones, fitness trackers, whatever. So not only can the device access all data from someone's home, but when you got home from work each day, it would connect to your mobile devices. It could see where you've been and when. It could also access stored passwords and network information from the places you've visited. You need to find out where this was installed. There's no telling what information has been compromised without the end user's knowledge. Think about it. If someone could set this up, and the user had access to classified sites like the Pentagon, you'd just given someone the roadmap to hack in undetected."

"Now who's acting like those guys from *The X-Files*?" Cameron replied, trying to lighten the mood, even though inside her heart felt like it was beating out of her chest. This was way out of her pay grade.

"The Lone Gunmen."

"Jesus, Casey, I'm not doing this with you again. There were three of them. More than one is not 'lone.' And that's beside the point. I got the info on the homeowner, and I'm on my way there now. The address is in Southampton. It's a summer home. His primary residence is in the city. Homeowner's name is Mark Minsky. I haven't had time to read the info I found on him. Can you google while I drive?"

"Sure, super easy." She could hear the clicking of his keyboard as he answered. "This guy has a Wikipedia page. Looks like old New York family money. The family owns a bank, and he's a venture capitalist. And there's our connection to Synergistic. He's a long-term investor. Looks like he's been giving them money since the start."

"A bank? Could someone use the chip for secure bank codes and passwords? Is this about a robbery?" She was so shocked by the implications that she almost missed her next exit.

"It's possible, and it may be the most probable of all the scenarios I've come up with. If he ever took a laptop back and forth from home to his office, he'd have lots of good info on it. Wanna rob a bank?" he joked.

"Ha ha." Blowing off the suggestion, she plowed on, picking up a little speed, her anxiousness in getting to her destination mounting. "Did you have a chance to look at any other hubs to see if this is an isolated incident?"

"I did. I didn't find any other chips, and I went through at least twenty units. I'll keep looking, but my best guess is that it's a one-off. The chip wasn't implanted during the manufacturing process. It was installed after. It may not be the only one out there, but it's not a widespread occurrence."

"Well, that's a relief, at least. Should we even be doing this, then? I mean, should I just reach out to the detective on the murder investigation, tell him what I know, and walk away?"

"Probably, but I'm still going to dig deeper into this chip. I want to see if I can trace where the data is being sent. What were you even going to do at the house, go talk to the guy?"

Cameron paused a few minutes before replying, knowing she was getting ready to cross a line and wondering how deep she should get Casey involved.

"Do you want plausible deniability?"

"Are you kidding? What's the plan?"

"I've got a Raspberry PI with that special software on it. I've also got his Wi-Fi password. I was going to do a scan and see all the devices associated with his network. It'll give us a complete picture of everything connected to his network and what sort of data has been compromised."

"How'd you get his Wi-Fi password?"

"Luckily, Barry's guys put in an extra SSID for his team to use when they're servicing all their accounts. They always use the same password. I saw it on a Post-it when I was in his office."

"Idiots. Well, turn off your phone and your tablet about a mile out from the property. You don't want any of your devices associated with the network. Even by accident."

"Gotcha. Look, traffic's a bitch. I might not make it out there until five or so. If you're gone for the day by the time I get this done, I'll just meet you at your office Wednesday first thing." She had two appointments scheduled for tomorrow she couldn't miss. "Can you e-mail me whatever additional info you find on the transmitter?"

"Sure thing, boss. Then after this, we go to the cops. It looks like this is an isolated incident. There's nothing else we can do."

"Agreed. Thanks, Casey. I know this isn't in your job description, and I appreciate you helping me out."

"No worries. This has been the most interesting part of my day. Though it was more fun when I thought we were dealing with a conspiracy. I'd stay late tonight and get really into this, but the baby's only a month old, and my wife needs the help."

"Do what you need to do, just don't take that thing home with you."

CHAPTER THIRTEEN

I'M LIKE A NINJA

CAMERON was frustrated. She'd been able to get into Mark Minsky's network, and gaining access to all his device information was a cakewalk. She'd done everything she'd told Casey she would, but she still hadn't moved her car from where she'd parked it. She'd pulled off on a strip of road that was maybe once a driveway for a piece of property connecting to the Minskys'. Or maybe it was for access to an old barn she saw up the way. Regardless, it wasn't important. What *was* important was the internal dialog she'd been having with herself the last ten minutes.

She was thinking about breaking into the house. It was an insane idea, but no matter how much she thought about it, she always ended up at the same conclusion.

She had to get inside.

Growing up, Cameron had always been a bit of a wild child. She'd cleaned up her act as an adult, and those days were long gone, but even in her wildest days, she'd never broken into a house.

She wanted the hard drive from his network video recorder, not just his network map. It was a stupid idea. She had no idea how much data storage he had, or how long the recordings were saved on the hard drive. It was most likely there would be no useful information to get, but she still couldn't talk herself out of it. What if the device was planted on-site? There could be a video of someone installing it.

During her initial scan of Mr. Minsky's network, she discovered he had cameras covering the whole property. Cameras she could tap into, but that would do no good. To access the stored data recordings on the hard drive, she'd have to physically take it. She knew where it was. The pictures in the *Hamptons Magazine* article gave a clear layout. She knew exactly where the NVR was located in the equipment rack and where it was in the house. She knew the model of the product, and a quick google search told her the hard drives were hot-swappable, so she wouldn't even need tools to get it out. She could do this.

The only issue was getting into the house itself. A quick check of the lighting and HVAC system confirmed no one was home at the summer house. He had smart locks, and while the access code wasn't available to her, she was sure the techs at Digital Lifestyles had them. She could call and get them, but they'd want to know why. And that would leave a trail, so that wasn't an option.

She could try to guess the code, but that would take forever, and she might never get it.

She checked the layout of the cameras on the blueprints she had. There was no way she would be able to approach that house without getting caught on at least one camera. No worries if she made it inside and got the hard drive; all evidence of her entry would be erased. But if she didn't, she'd be caught. Luckily, he didn't seem to have an alarm monitoring system set up, so at least the cops wouldn't be called if she did break in.

She had another idea. It was kind of crazy, but it could work. Though was it worth the risk? She wasn't a cop. She and Casey had done way more than most would just digging this far into the strange chip she found. But that's what happened, she supposed, when you put a mystery in front of a bunch of nerds. They couldn't wait to solve the puzzle.

She checked her laptop again, confirmed her suspicions, and took a deep breath. She knew she'd already made her decision.

Sliding out of her car, she popped the trunk and grabbed some equipment out of her cache of demo gear. She ditched her jacket, throwing it in the back seat, and swapped her heels for an extra pair of flats. Then she clicked the locks and started down the old path that would lead her behind the property. Like most houses in the Hamptons, Mark Minsky had invested heavily in large shrubs that surrounded his property, blocking it from prying eyes. Pretentiously manicured topiaries lined the whole estate.

The greenery thinned out once she reached the back and some maintenance sheds. She got down on her hands and knees and pushed through the dense foliage into the backyard. She had a scratch on her face and had dirtied herself up a bit but came through not too much worse for the wear. She wasn't dressed for cat burglary, but never in a million years did she think this would be where she'd end up when she got dressed that morning.

The yard was spacious, and over the landscaping, she got her first glimpse of the house. It was typical in that elegant, relaxed-coastal-living style all Hamptons houses were. He even had the requisite large ridiculous sculpture in the yard, she noted. His was a giraffe. Tall and absurd-looking in the middle of his vast ornamentation, it somehow reminded her of the topiaries. So contrived in their placement.

The problem was there was no cover to the house from her place stuck to the side of the maintenance shed. It was a wide-open space of perfectly trimmed lawn, done in a checkerboard pattern. It had to be at least the length of a football field. His monthly lawn maintenance bill had to be obscene. Once she stepped onto that lawn, there was no turning back. She either got the hard drive, or she was caught.

With a deep breath, she made her decision and sprinted toward the pool house with everything she had.

Cameron crashed into the back of the pool house panting, completely out of breath. She had to get back to the gym. Weekly yoga was obviously doing nothing for her cardio. Grass stuck to the bottom of her pants, and she was glad she'd switched to flats and left her suit jacket in the car. She was sweating enough as it was even though it was cool out.

She peeked out from around the building and spied a

door close to her on the long side of the pool. Taking a minute to catch her breath, she began making her way to the door.

Scurry, scurry, scurry.

Slide, duck, slide.

Back to the wall, ducking under the windows, crawling on occasion, she began humming the *Mission Impossible* theme in her head to try to alleviate some of her anxiety. She must look like an idiot, but if she got inside, she'd take the evidence and no one would ever see this stellar display of stupidity.

Reaching the back door, she took a look into the open-floor-plan living room and kitchen, searching for what she needed. She found it sitting on the kitchen countertop: a brand-new HTH. This was her Hail Mary. It was a shot in the dark, but if they had integrated the door locks into the entire system, she had a way to unlock the numeric keypad on the door without having the code.

She hesitated for a moment but realized it was far too late to back out. She'd for sure already been caught on camera. Regardless of her attempt to stay hidden, she knew her attempts at concealment crossing the yard were insufficient. So there was nothing left to do but more forward.

Closing her eyes to center herself for what she was about to do, she took a deep breath. Reaching into her backpack, she pulled out two devices: one, the laser from her fiber termination kit, the other a connecting device for her phone. Her phone that, per Casey's advice, she'd disconnected from both cellular and Wi-Fi access. It wouldn't ping off any local cell towers or connect to any network now.

She'd learned this trick from one of her dealers. Apparently, someone had discovered a hack using laser light to send audio signals to voice-controlled devices, and it worked over long distances. How it worked was well out of her paygrade, but she'd learned to do it. Thank God for bored AV techs who spent way too much time on YouTube.

She hooked it all together the way she was taught and pointed the laser in the direction of the HTH she could see through the glass door.

Here goes nothing.

She hit the button and calmly spoke into her phone. "AIME, unlock back door."

Please have named it "back door."

The hub lit up blue on the counter, meaning her command had been heard, and the lock before her flashed as well. In the silence of the afternoon, she heard the deadbolt turn and unlock the door. *Holy shit, it worked.* She made a mental note to buy the guys who taught her the trick a beer. They'd earned it. Now only one more hurdle before she could enter the house.

"AIME, alarm off." She waited a minute, and nothing happened.

So she tried again. "AIME, turn off alarm." That time she heard the corresponding beeping she associated with an alarm panel turning off.

She put her hand in her sleeve and pushed the now unlocked door open. She smiled. She was in.

And now she was officially a burglar.

CHAPTER FOURTEEN

GD COOKIE SEASON

ONCE inside the house, there was thankfully no more need for trying to sneak around. She strolled through the living room bold as you please to the hallway on the opposite side of the kitchen. She'd studied the magazine article to reference the floor plan in her search for the equipment room and determined it was in a closet off the hallway, but there were a lot of doors. She'd greatly underestimated the size of the house.

After a few rounds of trial and error, she found it behind the fourth door she opened. Bigger than she'd imagined, she was grateful the room was the size of a walk-in closet. A Hamptons-sized walk-in closet was way more spacious than a city-sized version, of course. She'd have room to work. Shutting the door behind when she entered, she flipped on the lights and surveyed the gear.

Taking in the scene, she was grateful for Digital

Lifestyles' dedication to making clean racks. The Minskys' system was impeccably built, and it had all the extras. Lots of fans for cooling, USB lights to plug in for delicate work, and a designated laptop for working on the system.

They almost made it too easy.

She logged into the laptop. They used the same password she'd used for the Wi-Fi. When all this was over, she was going to have a talk with Barry about security protocols for protecting his customers. But for now, she focused on the immediate need. She logged into the system programming and checked the notification settings on the NVR. Score, no one was set to receive motion notifications. That meant she'd gotten in clean; nobody would know she was there, and she could take her time. Well, theoretically, as long as someone wasn't watching the camera feed in real time. But the odds of that were slim, so she was reasonably sure she was okay. She disabled motion recording. The unit would continue to function for live viewing, it just wouldn't record, and nobody would notice the difference until they tried to pull up any stored footage. Hopefully, with no one being in residence at the summer house, that wouldn't be any time soon. At the very least, it'd be plenty of time for her to get out of the house, and that was all that really mattered.

She then set out to accomplish the task she'd come to do. Taking the Raspberry PI out of her bag, she plugged it into the network. Accessing the menu on the device, she opened the setting to scan for all ports and did a scan of the entire network, quickly collecting all data on his system and every device that had ever been connected to it. It would give her a complete blueprint of all technology in the house, everything the chip in the HTH would've had access to—just in case she missed anything in her remote scan. When they turned the info over to the police, it may help determine what whoever put it there had been looking for.

It was easy for Cameron to find the NVR. She quickly located the hard drive and removed it, then slid it into the backpack she brought with her. She zipped up the backpack and was preparing to leave when she saw it. An ethernet cable was running out of the NVR in a different direction than all the others. It didn't appear to connect to the POE switch that was powering the cameras. She traced it down and discovered an external hard drive. He must have added it for additional storage space. Sneaky, and she almost missed it. That would've been a disaster. All the evidence of her crime would've been stored there for anyone to see.

She was unhooking the external hard drive and preparing to remove it from the rack a melodic ringing echoed throughout the house. Someone had rung the doorbell. Cameron's heart skipped a beat and then began pounding in earnest. She could almost hear her heart as her fear had her frozen in place. She held stone still for what felt like forever but was most likely a minute at most. Not moving, barely breathing.

After a few minutes passed, she blew out a deep breath and began to relax. Everything was okay; they must have left. She reached back down to finish removing the drive.

Ding-dong.

There it went again. Whoever was at the door hadn't

gone away. She hoped it wasn't a neighbor or someone who had seen her sneaking through the yard and came to check it out. Reaching up, Cameron grabbed the laptop for the equipment rack and sat on the floor. She logged into the web viewer for the cameras and tried to find a clear view of the front door.

C'mon, she thought, clicking rapidly, *how many cameras can one house have?*

Searching through all the cameras in the system, she finally found the view of the front door and sighed in relief. It was a little girl with a woman Cameron could only assume was her mother. She recognized the familiar Girl Scout uniform; it must have been cookie time. She watched patiently from the floor of the equipment room until the little cookie pusher was on her way, waiting until the pair had made their way completely down the front drive before she made her move to leave. She grabbed her backpack with both hard drives off the floor, checked the computer once more to be sure she'd deleted all traces of her break-in, and casually left the property, locking the door behind her.

Her first crime was a success.

CHAPTER FIFTEEN

FIRST, YOU KNOW, WITH THE LAWYERS

MONDAY saw Detectives Justus back at the Synergistic offices, and he didn't have much enthusiasm about it. Partially because the ADA had insisted on coming with him instead of Alan and being in Kim Goodrich's company was an annoyance he never wanted.

Smartly dressed as always, without a hair out of place, Kim was an attractive woman. But what had always seemed to get in Will's way was her near-constant sour expression and the way her smiles never looked real. He didn't know what it would take to make Kim Goodrich laugh, like out-and-out belly laugh, and after their brief relationship, he didn't waste any thought on it anymore. When he saw her these days, her expression favored smirks and an air of superiority. If he were honest with himself, it did seem like a more natural fit, and he sometimes wondered why she even bothered faking when there were together. She couldn't be happy constantly putting on a front, or so he thought. He knew he couldn't live that way, and not for the first time, he wondered why she had even wasted so much of her time with him.

Will watched her hold that expression the entire elevator ride up to the office where their meeting was to be held. "Remember, this is an informal meeting only. We have no legal right to compel or detain them, so tread lightly."

Will fought to hold in his eye roll. Lawyers were never fun company, and today they would have two of them, plus Kim. They were there to interview the three remaining principals of Synergistic, and Will would've preferred to do it at the precinct. He and Alan had discussed it at length the previous day and grudgingly decided to conduct the initial interviews at SE. It offered them less control, but hopefully the familiar surroundings would make the principals more comfortable and more likely to share information. There was also the fact that, at this point in the investigation, they had no leverage to get them to the station, and if the suspects declined their invitation, they'd just end up at the SE offices anyway and lose the upper hand, as Kim had reminded him so very often on the trip over. Assuming they had the upper hand in the first place, which Will doubted very much. He also doubted the principals would say anything useful. But a lot could be learned by witnessing their dynamic. After researching the background of the people involved, Will had to admit he was interested in seeing how this group interacted with each other.

His suspicion grew as they were shown into Trey

Howell's office. The first thing he noticed was the size. It was larger than his apartment. It was professionally decorated and styled, but that didn't hold his attention. What struck him most was that the three occupants seemed to be professionally styled as well. From their positioning to their wardrobes, they could have been posing for a photo shoot. Evenly spaced throughout the room, they were staged in a way he couldn't fully explain, and he wondered if Kim noticed.

Trying to keep his preconceived notions about the group out of his head, he took his first real look at the technology icons who made up Synergistic Engineering.

Tall, dark, and handsome seemed a cliché made for Trey Howell. He was dressed in what Will assumed was his usual office wear: a graphic tee and jeans with a blazer. A sort of "I may be a suit, but I'm still cool" outfit. Will wasn't impressed; he could see through it and saw it was calculated. Designed to class it up enough for the business side and the press but not enough to isolate him from the technical staff. His marketing team probably crafted the look for him to keep him on brand.

He was sitting in a chair facing a couch, holding the hand of his VP of sales, Tessa Wells. Tears glistened in her eyes, and it was impossible to tell at first glance whether her grief was genuine or not. Will suspected not. She reminded him a bit of Kim, though he couldn't put his finger on why exactly. Both women were striking but in very different ways. Where Kim gave off a strong "don't mess with me" vibe, it seemed Tessa looked fragile, younger than her years—doll faced and innocent looking, even though he knew from her arrest records that she was a bit of a party girl and had seen her share of trouble. Looking at them, he felt a strange urge to rescue her. It was a misplaced notion, and in a moment of clarity, he realized what about her reminded him of Kim. It was the fact that it was all fake. A role she was playing. If that had anything to do with her guilt or innocence in this matter, he didn't know, but it was interesting nonetheless.

Trey and Tessa looked to be closer than coworkers, and from his research, he knew they had dated off and on in the past. Heads close together, Trey wiped a tear from her eye. Again, he found himself wondering just how much was real and what was for show. Looked like maybe they might be on again if the way she looked at him was anything to go by.

Brandon Reece, SE's in-house council, was standing at the window looking out onto the street. While the office was on the top floor of the building, it wasn't tall enough to have a view of the skyline in this neighborhood. He looked thoughtful as he turned to watch their entrance into the room. His face wasn't sad as far as Will could tell. He seemed more irritated or even angry. Will wondered what they'd been discussing before his arrival to put that look on his face.

Where Trey and Brandon were dark, Tessa was light. They had compiled a file on her background, and even though she looked every bit the damsel, she was quite an accomplished engineer in her own right. It wasn't hard to find information on her accomplishments. She had won a few awards for software development and engineering. Her résumé was as diverse and accomplished as any member of the staff. It seemed both Tessa and Trey had the skills to circumvent the security system and commit the murder. The only one in doubt was Brandon. He looked like the dumb jock, ex-football type, but dumb jocks didn't get law degrees from Harvard. It remained to be seen whether their lawyer had the technical know-how to pull it off.

Petite and waiflike, Tessa had moved and now sat delicately on the edge of the couch clutching a tissue and silently crying. It seemed a little much. They had all been notified of the murder on Saturday. Why now, three days later, was she crying? Was there more to their relationship than coworkers?

"You'll have to excuse us," Trey said, glancing at Tessa. "Emotions are a little high just now. We've just met with Matt's parents, and it was a little tough to take."

"Understandable," Will answered. "We'll try to be brief as we can. I'm Detective Will Justus, and this is Assistant District Attorney Kim Goodrich."

"A detective named Justus?" Brandon reacted with a smirk. Brandon was, it seemed, a lesser version of Trey. Still dark and good-looking, he was a little shorter, a little rounder, and a little less attractive. He wondered what, if any, role that played in the group dynamic.

"U-S, not I-C-E," Will replied with his standard answer every time it came up. At least now he knew who the comedian was in the room.

"I know you," Tessa said, looking at Kim. "You're Marcus Celli's wife. We met at the Met Gala last year."

"Yes, we did," Kim answered. "It's lovely to see you again. I'm just sorry about the circumstances."

Tessa nodded, and Will was, for the first time, thankful for Kim's presence. Hopefully her social climbing would help them smooth the waters.

"You're here to talk to us about Matt," Trey stated. "I'm not sure what we can tell you. We were all at my place in the Hamptons Friday night."

"I understand it was a company party," Will replied. "Did you notice Mr. Rodriguez's absence? Wasn't he supposed to be there as well?"

"He was," Trey answered. "And I did notice he was missing, but that wasn't unusual. He wasn't a social guy. He worked nonstop. I honestly assumed he'd arrive later in the evening, but he never showed."

"When was the last time any of you saw him?" Will asked.

"It was Friday." This time it was Brandon who answered. "The three of us cut out from work around noon to head on out to the Hamptons. We asked Matt to go with us, but he stayed at the office. That's the last time any of us saw him."

"You were all together then, during that conversation?"

"Yes," Trey replied. "We were heading out of the city and wanted to see if Matt wanted to ride with us to avoid Friday traffic."

"It's just so awful," Tessa said, maneuvering herself back into Trey's arms. "If we'd only insisted, he'd have come with us. He'd still be alive."

Trey patted her shoulder a few times and casually moved away. It was brief, but Will thought he caught a glimpse of fire, irritation at having been put off in her eyes as Trey moved away. Looked like Tessa wasn't getting the reaction from him she had hoped for.

"Do you have any leads?" Trey asked.

"I'm not at liberty to discuss that at this point in the investigation," Will answered. "I'd like to understand more about your security system. Who could've bypassed it?"

"Not many people," Trey replied, moving to place himself behind his desk. "We wrote the program ourselves, Matt, Tessa, and I."

"So any of you could've done it?" Will asked, cutting in.

"Of course," Trey answered smoothly "Though we'd have no need to. We all have full access over the building. It would take someone highly skilled to get past it. That combined with the destruction of all of our data makes me think this was corporate espionage."

"You think a rival company did this?" Will asked skeptically.

"Of course. It's the only thing that makes sense. Everyone was supposed to be at the party. That was public knowledge. Whoever broke in wasn't expecting to see Matt and panicked and killed him. It's the only thing that makes sense," Trey repeated.

It seemed unlikely to Will, but Kim was nodding right along. If it wasn't a targeted attack, then why were the only rooms in the entire office entered Matt's workspace and the server room? Someone hired for corporate espionage surely could've avoided Matt altogether. Seemed too likely a coincidence.

"Just to explore our options, can you tell me, did Mr. Rodriguez have any enemies?"

"Matteo?" Brandon replied, laughing. "No way. The guy was a total introvert. He spent most of his time working, and when he wasn't working, he was out with us. Everyone here liked him. All the programmers who worked for him thought he was a god."

"Did he have a girlfriend?" Will asked. The brief glance Brandon snuck at Tessa told Will everything he needed to know. "Ms. Wells, did you have a relationship with the victim?"

"It was over about a year ago," she answered, looking a bit flustered. "And I wouldn't exactly call it a relationship. We all hang around together, and a couple of times things just happened. We never really dated, and it only lasted a month or two."

"But you've dated Mr. Howell as well," he asked.

"Yes," she replied stiffly. "On and off since high school, though I'm not sure why that's relevant."

"Any jealousy there?" Will asked. He was poking at her, he knew it, but they hadn't felt the need for lawyers to step in yet. The two suits sitting at Trey's conference table hadn't spoken a word. They probably felt safe with Brandon there, but corporate law and criminal law were two very different things. And he wanted to unseat them a bit, see if they would squirm.

"Not on my part, I assure you," Trey answered smoothly.

"What Tessa and I had was always casual. She's one of my best friends, but there's no need for jealousy. If she and Matt were happy, then that made me happy, end of story."

This time Will knew he didn't imagine the rage that flashed in Tessa's eyes. It seemed she didn't think the relationship was so casual. But she got herself under control quickly and smoothed her features.

"Exactly. Casual." She almost spat the word out. failing miserably at feigning nonchalance. "No one here had a reason to kill him, least of all over a few indiscreet nights. We can provide you with a list of our rival companies. We've agreed it's your best place to start."

That made Will smile. They certainly knew where they wanted to point his investigation. This whole meeting had been staged.

He had to actively work to hide his grin now. They hadn't been very subtle and had given away more than they intended, he was sure. He could tell by looking at Trey that he realized it too, and this interview would soon be over. The next time he wanted to talk to any of them, it was going to be at the police station with their lawyers taking a more active role. But he could still get one last poke in before they left.

"And you, Mr. Reece, did you also share a few indiscreet nights with Ms. Wells?" he asked.

He got his answer not only by the red flush and accompanied stuttering nonanswer that Brandon Reece displayed, but also by the look of fury Tessa wore. It seemed Ms. Wells wasn't so good at hiding her emotions and had a bit of a temper.

"Will!" Kim exclaimed, admonishing him. Then she turned to Trey with a smile. "I apologize, Mr. Howell. That was uncalled for."

"Yes," he agreed, nodding his head, his tone calm and even. The epitome of a CEO. "I think this conversation has run its course. We'll provide you the list we discussed. Any further communication will have to be done through our attorneys."

Will didn't reply, just looked at the group, who, aside from Trey, seemed far less composed than they had been when they arrived. He was still trying to get a handle on the dynamic.

As soon as the elevator doors closed and they headed down to the lobby, Kim pounced on him.

"What was that about, Will?" she seethed, tongue between her teeth, reminding him of a snake. "We lost any chance of cooperation we had with them."

"We never were going to get any cooperation," he replied patiently, silently cursing the captain for requiring them to bring her along. "That whole thing was an act. One of them did it. They're just trying to point us in the wrong direction."

"How could you possibly know that?" she asked, her exasperation visible even through her Botox, face pinched and eyes squinted.

"How could you not?" he answered.

"Regardless of what your gut is telling you, there's this little thing called evidence. You have none. And I can't prosecute a case without it, so my advice is to follow up on that list and get me something I can use in court. Because you'll need a whole lot of something if you ever want to talk to those three again."

With that, the elevator doors opened into the lobby and she stormed off. Will's day was looking brighter already.

CHAPTER SIXTEEN

ANOTHER DAY, MORE REVENUE TOWARD QUOTA

TUESDAY for Cameron was kind of a bummer. Sitting in the SmartTech showroom in Manhattan pretending to pay attention to Keith Simmons, the showroom manager, present to the homeowners of the day was a little lackluster. It was a big project, and it seemed like Keith was having success at growing the SmartTech portion of the project, which was good for her and her quota. But she couldn't seem to get into it. She'd zoned out right about the point they were trying to decide between ivory and white for the keypads—so boring. She was still a little on a high from her B and E yesterday and wanted to get through this so she could have a chance to finish scanning through the data on the NVR's hard drives she had taken. She'd done a bit last night, but there were a lot of hours of recordings, and even fast-forwarding it was going to take some time to get through it all. Turned out Mr. Minsky had invested in as huge number of terabytes for storage and didn't often write over his data. She'd gotten more hours of recordings than she thought she would from those drives.

Keith had noticed her distraction, and he'd been giving her funny looks all morning. She was usually more involved, and she'd been leaning on him pretty heavily to carry the meeting this morning. Luckily, it seemed to be wrapping up, and she could take a few hours to work on her side project before her next meeting came in. It was fortuitous that both her clients today were scheduled for the showroom, so she didn't have to waste time running around getting to her appointments.

The SmartTech showroom, which had been a godsend for all the sales reps, was a perfect replica of an upscale Manhattan apartment in the front with offices and a conference room in the back. It made her life easier from a travel perspective for sure, but most important was the ability to demo all their products to the end users. Before, there had always been a disconnect between what the end users could understand about technology. Giving them an environment to actually see what they were buying and how it all worked together was a dream. And a huge boost to her commissions.

"So, what'd they decide?" she asked as Keith wrapped up the meeting.

"They couldn't. They're going to get the interior designer to pick. What's with you today?"

"Nothing, sorry. I didn't mean to check out there. Just

got a lot on my mind. I'm going to set up in the conference room and try to get some things done."

"Cool, I'll let you know when lunch gets here."

With his promise to order her a salad, she shut herself into the conference room and pulled out all the info she had discovered on Mark Minsky. She hooked up his hard drive to her laptop, popped open a Diet Coke, and began scanning through the footage.

She'd used the network topology she'd downloaded to discover the HTH had been installed roughly two months ago, which narrowed her search. She was trying to see if she could tell when it arrived or if it had been installed on-site. It was a long shot. Most likely he'd brought it into the house himself, and that would tell them nothing. It also wouldn't be visible since the garage where he parked his car was connected to the house, so she wouldn't be able to see him enter with it. And worst of all, he didn't have any cameras inside the house. His whole surveillance system was dedicated to the exterior of the property. Guess Mr. Minsky didn't want anybody seeing what went on inside.

But maybe, just maybe, it was a gift, and she would witness someone else bring in the hub. That would answer a lot of questions.

An hour later, she gave up. It was impossible. Two months ago was September, prime Hamptons season. Especially with the Labor Day holiday. Which meant the house that was rarely used now was Mr. Minsky's primary residence at the time. And man, he liked to party. Between the amount of people going in and out of the house and the number of cameras to sort through, she was never going to find anything. Breaking into the house had been a complete waste.

But there was a lot of other info to go through. As connected as people were these days, they had no concept of just how much information a person could get from them with very little effort. Most people were only concerned with identity theft. That should've been the least of their worries. The amount of data Mark Minsky produced was staggering. She could tell when he left and came home courtesy of his smart locks. She could tell when he was using the summer house in the Hamptons based on his smart thermostat settings. She knew when the maid came, what he watched on TV, and she had complete access to his computer's hard drive and his laptop when he brought it in the house. It was overwhelming. And possibly not even illegal. He had given his user info to Barry's company, Digital Lifestyles, and they did have a legal agreement to provide support for all their hardware. She was technically an employee, of a sort... after a fashion. It was a stretch, but it was possible that if anything ever came back from this, she could squeeze her way out of a felony charge.

Her dismay at her first foray into B and E and detective work being an abject failure was broken up by Keith knocking on the glass and holding up her lunch. She smiled and waved him in. She may not be cut out to be a spy, but she could still enjoy her Cobb salad.

The comfortable routine of sitting around the conference table having lunch with Keith began to snap her out of her funk.

"I haven't seen you in a while," she said between bites. "How's it going?"

"Good. It's been busy. Attendance is way up, so Steve's been happy."

"Freakin' Steve."

"Yep, freakin' Steve. I wish you were here last week for this one meeting I had. You would've died."

"Why, what happened?"

"It was awesome. A dealer brought in a customer. Oil guy, tons of money, and a much, much younger wife. I can't stress this enough. She could've been his granddaughter."

"What's weird about that?" she replied. She could see the humor in his eyes, holding back laughter. "That describes half the customers who come in here."

"It was so great." Chuckling to himself, he continued. "The wife left after a bit, and as soon as she was gone, the husband asks me if there's anything we won't integrate with. I ask him to be more specific, and he says a scale."

"So what? He wants to get notified if his wife's gained weight? What a dick."

"No, it's even better. It's so much better than that. Turns out he bought one of those gigantic scales like the veterinarian or the zoo would use to weigh animals. He's putting it under his bed. He travels a lot. He wants to set it up under his bed so if the scale measures more weight than what they've programmed for his wife, it will send a notification to his phone. He was really happy when I told him it could be done."

"What the fuck? So he's trying to catch her cheating? There are easier ways than that. Hasn't he heard of cameras? Also, the potential for false notifications is huge. Do they have a dog? What if it hops up on the bed?"

"I mentioned that. The wife has a bichon frise. They'll adjust the weight limit accordingly. They don't think the cat will make a significant enough difference to register. And he doesn't want cameras in his bedroom… privacy concerns," he replied with a little smirk.

"Small dick?"

"I'd guess that or performance issues considering his age."

"Unbelievable. Just when I think people can't surprise me anymore," she said, shaking her head in disgust. "That's got to be a miserable marriage. I give it a two-year max."

"It won't last the year. You didn't see the wife."

The wife.

Something jogged in Cameron's brain. In all the video she had watched of Mark Minsky's house, there was one thing she'd never seen: his wife.

CHAPTER SEVENTEEN

YOU SAY POTATO, LET'S CALL THE WHOLE THING OFF

"IT'S the wife," she exclaimed as soon as Casey answered the video call. She and Keith had cleaned up their lunch, and she was alone again in the conference room.

"Well, hello to you too. Seriously, Cam, manners. You never call and say, 'Hi, how are you?' You just jump right in."

"Hi, how are you? It was the wife." She rolled her eyes, not caring that he could see her. "I watched so much of the stored data from his cameras, and he's never with his wife. Lots of other women but never her. So, I looked it up. Seems like she lives overseas. What do you want to bet they're getting a divorce and she's looking for leverage?"

"I don't buy it. She's his wife. She wouldn't have to resort to this to get that kind of info. If she wanted his video recordings, she could just walk into the house and take them.

Plus, it's kind of a sophisticated maneuver for a woman who basically shops for a living." He caught her side-eye in the monitor. "Yeah, I looked her up too. Don't look so surprised. And if she just wanted dirt on him with other women, she didn't have to do any of that. There's plenty info on *Page Six* to do the job. Also, she's been living overseas for years."

"Fine, it's not the wife. It's not a conspiracy. What's your brilliant idea, genius?"

"It's a heist," he answered confidently. He looked so excited at the prospect that he was bouncing a bit in his seat behind his desk.

"How'd you get there?" she asked. "Tell the truth, you just wanted to say the word heist."

"I've been examining the protocol on the chip you found. It does exactly what I said it did with one additional wrinkle." He paused in his speech, still bouncing, obviously excited about what he found. He wanted her to ask, she could tell. So she purposely waited to see how long he could contain himself. She didn't have to wait long. "Aren't you going to ask?"

"What did you find?" She smiled a bit to herself, lips tipping up at the corners, his excitement contagious.

"There's a priority protocol written into the program."

"Huh?" She didn't see what he was getting at.

"There's obviously minimal storage on the device. That's why it sends the data every night. It's also why I couldn't find any of the previous data. It erases everything after it's sent. So I looked a little deeper into the code. If the device takes in too much data on a given day, priority is given to information collected from certain devices. It isn't any of his smart home gear. Priority is given to computers, laptops, and tablets."

Her brain swirled with this new information, gathering the data presented and making the logical conclusion. "So that's what they're after. Data. Specifically, Minsky's data. They don't care about his surveillance system, or when he gets home every day. They want whatever he has on his computers. And you think because his family owns the bank and he's a money guy that it's a heist. Why couldn't it be simpler than that? Why couldn't someone just be using the information gathered to manipulate the stock market? I'm sure there's a way you could make money there, and with considerably less risk."

Casey's face fell. She'd burst his bubble. "Well, sure, you could do that. But my version is way more fun."

Cameron laughed. "True, so, okay, we'll keep heist in the mix. But I think my idea is more plausible. Which means this has nothing at all to do with Matt Rodriguez's death. I'm sorry, Casey, I sent us on a wild-goose chase.

He shrugged. "Nothing to be sorry about. It's been fun. And you're probably right, but manipulating the stock market is illegal as hell. We'll still have to contact the authorities. Although now I'm not sure which authorities. The NYPD detectives investigating Matt's murder or the SEC?"

"I wouldn't begin to even know how to contact the SEC. Unless we contact that client I insulted."

"I remember that. Didn't you think he worked for the

South Eastern Conference?"

"I'm from Kentucky," she snapped. "He just said SEC. It was a logical assumption." And embarrassing as hell when he corrected her. "We'll stick with the NYPD like we planned. I'll come out to the office first thing in the morning and pick up the units. I'll turn them in myself and explain it to them."

"You still have to tell Steve."

"I know, but at least this way, it isn't some vast global conspiracy involving SmartTech. He won't care as long as it doesn't affect profits."

"True, but we are forgetting one thing. There is another possibility."

"Oh yeah, what's that?

"Beta test."

"Beta test?"

"Yes, beta test. This could be Synergistic themselves. This could be a beta test to see if the system would work with large-scale distribution. Can you imagine?"

She could imagine, and it was horrifying. A company like Synergistic, with the global reach it had, having access to that much data? It was definitely the worst-case scenario. She shook herself out of those thoughts before she went down that rabbit hole.

"All the more reason to turn over the chip and the info. We're not qualified for this. We've done way more than enough. It's time to let it go."

"Agreed. I'll see you in the morning, then.

"Yep, see you then," she replied and hung up.

She tried to put it out of her mind, but the idea Casey had planted stayed with her and grew as she got herself prepared for her next meeting. Any way she looked at it, a company like Synergistic with all that information was the stuff of nightmares.

CHAPTER EIGHTEEN

BACK TO THE OFFICE

WEDNESDAY morning, Cameron was back on the road again at what for her was still early. To other people, it was 10:00 a.m.. After finding out the situation with the hub was a one-off, she'd relaxed a bit and didn't feel like she had to meet Casey at the office first thing. She could take her time to answer some emails and wait for traffic to die down before traveling back to New Jersey.

Casey never sent her any new info on the chip the previous evening, so she spent her night researching Mark Minsky some more. She wanted more than the cursory info she'd gotten on Monday's drive out to his place. He was young, thirty-six years old. Just like Trey Howell. Born in Manhattan, he grew up in boarding school, a roommate of Trey's. The two had been good friends since then. It was amazing what could be discovered on the internet. Especially if you were a rich New York socialite and had been mentioned on Socialite Rank in your younger days. People really didn't realize whatever you put on the internet was there forever. Thank God for cached websites. Seemed as if Mr. Minsky ran with quite the party crowd during that site's heyday. There were still links to all the photos and gossip for her to find.

It was amazing. She was almost the same age as Mark Minsky and his crowd, but their lives were vastly different.

Parking in the lot, Cameron jumped out of her Jeep and straightened her clothes. Being five feet four and driving an SUV was always a little bit of a jump for her, but it was the only kind of car she'd ever owned. Albeit her brand-new model with only seven thousand miles on it was a far cry from her brother's hand-me-down that she drove in high school, but she'd loved Jeeps then as much as she did now. She was again dressed in a suit, but the weather in the northeast was beginning to turn chilly as they headed into late November, so she grabbed her coat and her messenger bag out of the car and headed into the building to Casey's office. She'd typed up all the info she had the night before, but she wanted to add his and take it to the detective in charge of the case. That way she could clear her conscience.

She knew something was wrong the moment she walked into the lobby. It took a beat before she realized what struck her as different. The music was off. Generally, they had some cheesy Muzak background music piped in, but today, without it, the silence in the lobby seemed unnaturally loud. Echoes of whispers and footsteps sounded cold and uncomfortably loud against the marble floors and glass-enclosed lobby. There was an unusual number of employees congregating in the open entrance space. Grouped together, talking, hugging. But it was the phones that caught her attention. The persistent ringing of unanswered phones. She saw Melissa, the SmartTech receptionist, wiping tears from her face and made her way over to her.

"What's going on? Why's everyone freaking out?"

"Oh, Cameron, it's just terrible. We just got the news. Casey Keane was in a horrible car accident on the way to work today. He's dead."

The world seemed to fall away in that instant. Her vision narrowed. All the noises and movement seemed to turn into one big blur, and focus was impossible. She had to force herself to breathe before she passed out.

Casey was dead? It was unbelievable. She talked to him every day. He couldn't just be gone. Her eyes grew moist, and she had to blink back tears. Not Casey, her friend who'd been having so much fun playing at solving a mystery with her this week.

"What happened?" Cameron asked, suddenly suspicious, a chill running down her spine. The timing was just too coincidental for her liking. *Patience*, she told herself. Car accidents happened all the time; it didn't mean it was deliberate. He'd had the hub for the last two days, and nothing had happened. Hell, she'd had it over a weekend and was fine. But what if? If it was still transmitting, what might the person on the other end have learned?

"Hit-and-run," she answered. Melissa had been with SmartTech for over ten years. Normally she was the office gossip and a fount of information, but this news seemed to quell the natural boisterousness in her. She was more subdued than Cameron had ever seen her. Melissa was a tough girl, tattooed, and always with a different color dye in her hair. Nothing usually seemed to faze her, but apparently death did. "I saw it, you know? On my way to work, I passed an accident on the Palisades. A burned-out car in one of the lanes. I was pissed. It was down to one lane, and I felt like it was going to make me late to the office. How selfish is that?"

"You didn't know. That's what everyone thinks when they see an accident," Cameron said. But her mind was racing with what to do next. She had to call Bill and Phil and let them know. They'd be devastated too. They loved Casey as much as she did. And she had to get the chip. She had to turn it over to the police before it disappeared or got someone else hurt.

"He just had a baby. Like a month ago. I can't imagine what his wife must be thinking."

"It'll be okay, Mel. God only gives us what we can handle," Cameron repeated the platitude she'd heard so many times when her father died, but as with hearing it then, it just felt hollow to say. Nothing people could say could make you feel better in a time like this. But for Cameron, being proactive helped. She'd put her focus on getting the chip to the police and put Casey out of her mind for now. She'd deal with her grief later.

Never being good in these kinds of situations, Cameron was trying to do what she could to sound concerned while simultaneously trying to extract herself and make her way to Casey's office, but she couldn't just leave Melissa there crying. Her opportunity came when a girl from marketing came over to commiserate as well. She took that as her chance to escape and made her way up the stairs as quickly as she could without running and drawing attention to herself.

The scene was the same upstairs as it had been in the lobby, but she successfully dodged everyone and made it to Casey's office. The door was shut, and with a glance around to make sure no one was looking, she cracked it open and ducked inside.

With the lights off and the blinds drawn, it was hard to see in Casey's office. This was the first time she'd been grateful for his lack of accoutrements. She immediately rushed to his desk and began searching the top. Nothing but files. She moved to the drawers, which proved more challenging to search. Like a true nerd, his drawers were full of miscellaneous cables and parts. It took her several minutes, but she was unsuccessful in finding the chip there as well. She turned to the shelves on the wall and immediately spotted the two HomeTech Hubs she left with him. Cursing herself for not checking there first, she grabbed the first box and discovered what she'd been looking for. The rogue chip sat right on top of the interior packaging. She grabbed it and shoved it in her bag, glad, not for the first time, that she always carried monster-sized bags, and it would fit along with all her other gear. She made her way back to the door, checked to see no one was looking, and slipped out.

Back in her Jeep in the parking lot, she took several deep breaths and thought about her next move.

Holy shit, holy shit. Casey is dead.

The device was in her possession now, and if what Casey said yesterday was true, it would transmit whatever data it collected at midnight. That gave her thirteen hours and some change before anyone would know someone had taken it. She didn't know enough about it to know if it would connect with the Wi-Fi in her car, or if this chip could use that to identify her, but she didn't want to take any chances. It was well past time to hand this over to the police. Maybe if she'd done that yesterday, Casey would still be alive.

She had to try hard to not travel down that path; most likely it was just an accident. She couldn't be certain his death was related, but she couldn't ignore it either. Who was receiving these transmissions, and what had they heard from Casey that was so threatening they'd had to kill him?

One thing was certain: if someone murdered Casey, then the odds of this not being connected to Matt Rodriguez's death were slim to none.

She pulled out her phone and googled Matteo Rodriguez. Scrolling through the hits, she found the *New York Times* article on the murder, which listed the detective on the case as a William Justus. She snorted. *Justus. What a ridiculous name for a detective.* She saw he worked out of the 10th precinct. She looked up the number, called, and was immediately shut down. Being a sales rep had given Cameron a lot of experience trying to get around gatekeepers, but the woman on the other end of the line was immovable. No, she could not connect her to the detective; she didn't know if he was in; she didn't know where he was. The best she could do was take a message.

Frustrated, Cameron ended the call and drove into the city. She parked her car at the garage in her apartment building, made a quick detour, and then walked to the Midtown South precinct on 35th Street.

CHAPTER NINETEEN

YOU NEVER GET A SECOND CHANCE…

SITTING on the bench in front of the police station, Cameron waited for Detective Justus. She'd had time to think during her drive into the city and decided this was her best bet of meeting the man. Surely he'd have to return to his office at some time.

It was cold in the city that Wednesday, fall having begun to turn to winter. She'd grabbed a coffee on her way to warm her during her wait, but it wasn't doing the trick. Her mind kept drifting to Casey's accident, and those thoughts were chilling. She made a difficult call to Bill and Phil, and as predicted, they were devastated. She spent the rest of her time on the hard city bench between calls and emails from her customers and researching the players involved. She'd found a picture online of Detective Justus, so she'd recognize him when he arrived. She had also researched his background—what she could find, anyway—discovering he was a native New Yorker and had been in the military. He didn't have any social media profiles, so information was hard to come by.

Information on Synergistic and the partners there was much easier to find. She'd found dozens of pictures of them at different parties and social events. Trey Howell always featured prominently, as well as their attorney, Brandon Reece, and the VP of sales, Tessa Wells. From what she could see, the three of them plus Mark Minsky had been friends since they were kids. The boys all attended the same boarding school near Boston. She found pictures of them in their youth, parties, vacations, and hunting trips. The pictures ran the gamut, but the common thread was they lived a luxurious lifestyle. She wasn't sure where Tessa came in, but as a native New Yorker, she'd probably run in the same circles as the boys.

Cameron had been sitting in front of the precinct for almost three hours and her fingers felt frozen by the time she saw Detective William Justus walking up the street with an older man. Her first thought was that his pictures didn't do him justice—pun intended. He was hot. She'd expected Columbo but had gotten Rockford instead. While not a classically handsome man, his presence was arresting. He was attractive in a way she couldn't quite explain. While he was tall, dark, and broad-shouldered, his face wasn't particularly pleasing, at least not in a conventional sense. A mix of features that individually may not have worked, but somehow on his face, they seemed just right. There was something about the way he carried himself that was undoubtedly masculine. To a woman like Cameron, who spent her days with men who didn't even watch sports, it was almost overwhelming.

She'd just about let him walk past her before she had the presence of mind to shove her iPad into her bag and stand up to address him.

"Detective Justus?" she asked tentatively, trying to get his attention. Nothing. So she said it louder. "Detective Justus?"

"Yes," he answered, turning to face her.

"You're the detective in charge of the Rodriguez murder," she stated, glancing between the men. She recognized the man with him as Detective Alan Jones, his partner. Both of them grew noticeably cautious at her statement.

"Yes. How can we help you?" His words were kind but guarded.

"My name's Cameron Caldwell. I think... well, I think I know why Mr. Rodriguez was killed." She could tell they were doubtful. Her assumption was confirmed when Detective Jones spoke next.

"Did you kill Mr. Rodriguez?"

"What? No. Jesus. Look, I work in sales for a tech company. I found something in one of the HomeTech Hubs last Friday. I showed it to a coworker, and now he's dead. Trust me, I can help you."

Detective William Justus gave her a long, hard look before speaking. So much so that Cameron became nervous, shuffling her weight between her feet on the Manhattan sidewalk. Maybe coming to the police wasn't a great idea.

Perhaps she should've gone to Steve and just let her boss decide how to handle it.

"Well, why don't we get inside, out of the cold, and you can tell us about it."

CHAPTER TWENTY

INTERVIEW? INTERROGATION?

CAMERON saw the skeptical look Will shared with Alan as they walked into an interrogation room on the third floor of the precinct. At least she assumed it was an interrogation room. Dark and cold. Though not as cold as outside. Gray, dingy walls and a hard metal table were the first things in the room she noticed. She grew more nervous the longer the detectives' silence went on. They'd gestured for her to sit in the hard metal chair at the table but hadn't said a word since.

She decided whatever game they were playing by not speaking didn't matter. Whatever happened to Casey was way more important than playing dominance games with a pair of detectives. She'd seen enough of those with the guys at work. She needed to know more than anything if Casey's death really was an accident.

She spoke hesitantly at first, then grew in confidence as

her story unfolded. She told them about finishing her regular workday on Friday, visiting Barry at Digital Lifestyles, and her discovery of the chip in the HTH later the next morning. Then she shared the info she got from Casey, her discovery of the person who'd had the chip in his house, their suspicions, and finally of the death of her friend. She was thorough in her exposition, only leaving out the details of her adventure at Mr. Minsky's house from her tale.

When she was finished talking, Will and Alan shared a look. She could tell they weren't convinced. Part of her didn't blame them. Wasn't it just yesterday she'd been talking to Casey about how insane conspiracy theories sounded?

"So, let me see if I have this straight. You found spyware in an HTH that was installed in Mark Minsky's home?" Alan questioned.

"Yes."

"And at that point, you didn't think to report it to the police?"

"And tell them what? At that point, I didn't know it was spyware. I didn't know what it was. If it was an additional piece or if it was part of a new version that may have been added in manufacturing. I didn't know what it did until I took it to Casey, and we just found out the day before yesterday."

"And this morning he was in a car accident in New Jersey?"

"Yes. I don't have many details, but everyone in the office said it was a hit-and-run. He died on his way to work."

"How can that be related?" Will asked. "How could anyone know he'd discovered the spyware and act that quickly?"

"When Casey called me about the device, he confirmed it's a transmitter. It takes all the information and all the data of any device on the same network and transmits it at midnight every night. We assumed when we removed it from the HTH, it would no longer transmit, as Casey didn't connect it to the wireless network at the office, but that must not be the case. This thing is way more advanced than we thought. It must've automatically connected to an open network. If it did that, it could get the ID from the phones and tablets, the computers, the network, anything nearby. It wouldn't be a jump for them to discover who had the device. And even more, it would've been able to connect to all the devices on the network and see the tests he'd been running and know it had been discovered."

"Would they know you had it?"

"Yes. When I took it from Barry, I kept it in my apartment all weekend before delivering it to Casey. It could've connected to a nearby network and transmitted. But that's not suspicious. I was just a sales rep transporting a defective product to my tech support. Nothing compromising was done until Casey began running tests on it. I also never discussed anything related in front of the chip just in case. We never communicated via email or text regarding this. Just a couple of cell phone calls that, if they were overheard, were primarily about my knowledge of the failure of the hub to integrate with SmartTech Home Automation and my intention to deliver it to Casey. Until this morning, there was no reason to suspect anyone but Casey and I knew what the device really did."

"Until this morning?"

"Yes. After I heard about Casey's death, I took the chip from his office."

"Did you bring it here?" Alan asked.

"No, I hid it. I didn't want to bring it to the police station in case this isn't related to your case. I didn't want to tip anyone off. That should be your decision. But regardless, when the hub transmits tonight, whoever is receiving the data will know I took it."

"We could take it somewhere it can't transmit," Will said.

"Where?" Cameron asked. "I thought of that. I don't know all the specifics on how this thing works, and I'm not qualified to find out. All I can assume is that it'll connect to any network in range and transmit. We're in Manhattan. There is nowhere you can go that doesn't have a network. And though most are secure, there is always some idiot who leaves theirs open. Had I had some time, I could've maybe tried to get a wireless jammer to put with the hub to block transmission or get a Faraday box, but I didn't have time for that. I didn't want to leave it at the office. If Casey's death was deliberate, I didn't know if whoever's responsible would come looking for it. The way it's designed, you can pinpoint its location anywhere. Look, it won't transmit until midnight." She checked her watch. "That means you have eight hours to decide what to do with it."

"Before we do anything, will you explain to me why you think this is related to the Rodriguez murder?" Will asked.

"I'm not sure it is. I just have a hard time believing this is all coincidence. I guess I'm making a few assumptions based on what I know. First, someone planted spyware in Mark Minsky's home. A device that's concealed in and designed to use one of SE's HomeTech Hubs. The device is removed from the home, and the inventor of the HomeTech Hubs is killed. I have to ask myself, 'Is this the only hub that has spyware built in? Was Matt Rodriguez involved in this? Did he find out, and that's why he was killed?' I have way more questions than answers for you. And maybe you guys have found another reason someone might want the guy dead, I don't know. But I'd bet it's related. This device is very sophisticated. It would take someone extremely technical to program something like this. They'd have to have access to both SE and Mike Minsky to plant it. He's one of SE's initial investors. It can't be a coincidence. And with Casey's death this morning... something else is going on here."

"Okay, sit tight. We're going to check this out, and we'll be right back. Do you want a water or coffee or anything while you wait?" Alan said.

"No, I'm good, thanks," she replied, and they walked out of the room.

CHAPTER TWENTY-ONE

CUTE?

AS soon as the door to the interrogation room closed, Will shut his eyes and leaned against the wall, sighing audibly. "You think she's legit?" he asked his partner.

"I think she's scared as hell, and I don't think she's lying, but I'm not convinced it's related."

"You have to admit, it's an interesting wrinkle. We haven't been able to find any reason for anyone to want this guy dead. If he was spying on his investors and they found out? Or what if that's how Trey got him to invest? Blackmailed him, then killed Matt when he found out? It does pose a lot of questions."

Alan nodded. "I agree we can't ignore the possibility. What do we do about the chip? Do we bring it here and tip off whoever is receiving the transmissions?"

"I think we have to. We'll get our tech people on it. See if they can shut it down before it transmits tonight. I don't know if we can bring it here. Would that give them access to everything on our network? That would be a disaster. Jesus, this is why I hate technology."

"I agree. I'll call Doug Pernick in the tech department and get him to go pick it up with me from wherever she hid it. I'll explain the situation to him and see what his suggestion is. I'd love to find out where it's transmitting to."

"Okay, in the meantime, I'll see if she has any other info she can provide before I send her home."

"Uh-huh," Alan said with a knowing grin.

"What? If this information is accurate, she'll have proven to be exceptionally useful. We had nothing on this case an hour ago. The interviews with the SE people got us nowhere. Tracking down their competitors has been a bust. Corporate espionage, my ass. Plus I'll be happy to have something to report to Gil. Last night's update felt like pulling teeth."

"She's cute too."

"Cute? Shit, Al, she's a witness." It was a brush-off, but Will agreed. She was cute. Tough too. Even in the face of her friend's death, she had the wherewithal to stash the chip and come see them. She could've just tossed the thing and walked away.

"Yep, a cute witness. Didn't see a ring either." He winked, opening the door to the interrogation room, again halting Will from being able to reply. "Where'd you hide the chip, Ms. Caldwell?"

"Storage locker at Grand Central. Here's the info," she answered, passing a piece of paper and a key over to him.

Alan took it and headed out the door.

CHAPTER TWENTY-TWO

COPS INTERROGATIONS ARE NOT LIKE INTERROGATING THE UNIVERSE

DETECTIVE Will Justus had grilled her for another hour. But he was nice about it. She went through every detail of her weekend, several times over, to the point that she was getting turned around. She learned he was a little technophobic, and trying to get him to grasp the amount of data a person could get with this technology was a challenge. She thought she finally got him when she explained to him how she could rob a bank with the information she could get from Mark Minsky's devices. Either that or he thought she might actually be trying to rob a bank.

After their meeting/interrogation, she felt relieved. This whole situation was out of her hands now. The police could certainly take it from here. They had good tech people on staff, and she was sure they'd get to the bottom of this.

It was just too bad it was too late to help Casey. She'd

managed not to think too much about his death during the interview, but stepping out of the precinct beneath the darkening sky, she felt the grief suddenly hit her. Casey was dead. It was almost impossible to get her head around it. In her five years with SmartTech, Casey had been a lifeline for her. He'd grudgingly helped her learn how to navigate the company's tech support department when she first got hired, and he was her first point of contact for any help she needed. It was hard to imagine SmartTech without Casey, and even harder to imagine it was her fault he was gone. She'd brought him into this mess, after all.

She tried to keep it in perspective. It wasn't her fault. She didn't kill him. If anyone did. It still could've been an accident. Detective Justus said he'd reach out to the New Jersey police handling the case to see what they'd discovered, but it would take time to learn anything.

She took a detour on her walk home from the police station to hit her favorite Mexican restaurant for some takeout. The place was jumping. As she sat at the bar sipping a margarita she barely tasted, she never felt more disconnected. All these people and she'd never felt more isolated, like a ghost in the city.

When she got to her building, she said hi to the doorman. He'd been working in the building longer than she'd lived there. He'd introduced himself to her when she moved in, and she'd promptly forgotten his name. He never said it again, and after all these years, she was too embarrassed to ask.

She was feeling progressively worse after riding the

elevator to the eighth floor and getting off to head into her apartment. She unlocked the door and opened it to disaster. Her apartment had been ransacked. She only saw the living room, but everything was trashed, her TV shattered, couch cushions on the floor and shredded, pictures pulled off the walls. So much destruction.

Something shiny on the floor caught her eye, and she glanced down. It was a picture from her bedroom, frame bent and glass shattered everywhere. Bending down, she gently pulled the photo out of the mess. It was a shot of her, Bill, and Phil at a corporate event in Denver her second year with SmartTech. She remembered it vividly. It was a great night when she was just finding her stride within the group. To see it treated so callously was heartbreaking. The cherry on top of a real shitty day she just didn't need. She shook the glass dust off and slid the picture into her bag.

Without going inside, she shakily returned to the elevator, rode down to the lobby, and called the number on the card Detective Justus had given her.

He answered the phone with an amused lilt to his voice. "Calling so soon?"

"My apartment has been broken into."

"Don't go in. I'm on my way."

"Don't you need to know where I live?" she asked, then realized he'd hung up before she'd finished talking.

CHAPTER TWENTY-THREE

CAMERON'S PLACE

CAMERON tried to imagine what Will was thinking when he walked into her building and saw her perched on the reception desk sharing guacamole and chips with the doorman. His face gave away nothing as he took her in munching on her snack. She hoped he couldn't see the anxiety on her face as she tried to be casual with the doorman and the relief in her eyes when she saw him arrive.

"Have you been inside?" he asked as he walked over to them

"No," she replied. "I saw the mess when I opened the door and immediately came back down here."

"Good. Was the door locked?"

"Yes, I had to unlock it."

Will turned his attention to the doorman, who had stood at his approach. "Detective Will Justus," he said, reaching out to shake the man's hand.

"Joe Vestin," he replied by way of introduction.

Joe, she thought and repeated it to herself several times, trying to make the name stick.

He was a tall, sturdy-looking man with sharp features and a calm manner. "I've been with this building for twenty years. We've never had a break-in before. I've been here all day. I didn't see anyone suspicious come in. We call up when any nonresident enters the building."

"Is there another entrance?"

"Two more. A service entrance in the back, and the elevator goes directly to the garage downstairs, but you need a key to use it."

"Show me," Will demanded.

They all took a quick walk around the main floor and the garage, Joe pointing out the exits.

"Were you away from your desk at any time?" Will asked.

"Yes, twice that I can recall. Once when the UPS deliveries came in. I met the driver and brought all the packages to the package room. And again when I helped one of our older residents to her apartment on the sixth floor with her groceries. We also have security cameras. But I checked. The recordings from today have been erased."

"Whoever it was is probably gone," the detective commented, turning his attention back to her. "What time did you leave today?"

"I left at nine this morning for the office. I came back around twelve thirty to park my car before heading to hide the chip and then on to the police station to wait for you, but

I didn't go upstairs."

"Okay, I'm going to head up and check it out. I've called in a crime scene team. If they arrive before I come back, please send them up."

With that, Will walked away from them and boarded the elevator with her keys.

CHAPTER TWENTY-FOUR

FISH AND CHIPS, AND HOTELS

"OKAY, the crime scene team is going to be awhile," he said when he came back down. She'd sent the crew that had arrived up to meet him maybe ten minutes before. "How about you ditch the chips, and you and I can grab some dinner while they check things out? Talk about this a little more?"

She quickly agreed, not wanting to sit in the lobby to wait for them to do their work. She left her remaining guacamole and her tacos with Joe, who seemed to be enjoying them, and followed the detective.

The walk over to the restaurant was quiet and thoughtful, much like the city seemed that night. Light traffic on the streets and the chill in the brisk air. Nights like this were one of the reasons she'd come to love the city so much. It wasn't what was advertised, but the city could be so peaceful sometimes. A calming presence and a sense of familiarity she appreciated after her emotional day.

An awkwardness that wasn't present on their walk seemed to settle in once they were in a booth at her favorite Irish pub. The silence grew more pronounced as they sat, both perusing their menus. Cameron wasn't hungry anymore, and nothing looked good. In fact, she was barely seeing the menu. The break-in at her apartment had shaken her up more than she would like to admit. She wasn't a native New Yorker, but she'd always felt safe in her apartment. Before moving to the city, she'd researched neighborhoods in depth. Gramercy Park was a notoriously safe area, and living in a building with a doorman added to her feelings of security.

It was only now that she was realizing if someone wanted in, they could get in no matter where you were. The question was why? Never being able to stand long silences, she decided to broach the subject with the detective.

"I don't understand why someone would break into my place. Were they looking for the chip?"

Will started to answer but was interrupted by the waitress.

"What can I get for you two?"

"I'm not hungry," Cameron stated.

Will took her measure, then turned to the server. "Fish and chips for both of us. I'll have a Guinness. You want a beer?"

Cameron looked shocked that he'd ordered for her but recovered quickly. "Sure. Blue Moon?"

"Got it. I'll get that in for you now." The waitress smiled and walked away.

"I know you're upset, but you need to eat." She just nodded in response. "If I had to guess, I'd say you're right. Someone was searching for something. Unless there's another reason somebody would be in your place, I'm going to assume this is about the chip."

"It makes sense, I guess. It's just so fast. If we assume your murderer is also responsible for what happened to Casey, they must have discovered he'd identified the chip and knew what it could do. Since it only transmits once every day, the last time they could've tracked it would have been last night, when it was at the SmartTech office. They must've searched for it there and not found it. Maybe they can even ping its location anytime they want. Who knows? We can also assume it had been transmitting all weekend, so they'd know I was the person who took it from the Digital Lifestyles office and delivered it to SmartTech. It would be likely for them to assume I'd be the only other one aware of it and that I'd have it now. They probably wanted to get it before it could be delivered to the police. Did your team get it?"

"They did," he answered, taking his first sip of beer that the waitress had just dropped off. "I got a message from Al earlier. Our tech guys are working on it now. They're going to try to find a way to track the transmissions to see if they can't find out who's behind all this. But even if they can't, somebody will get a big shock tonight when they discover their device is in the hands of the police." He smiled.

"Hopefully that'll get them to leave me alone. There's no reason to go after me if I don't have the chip," she responded thoughtfully as she removed the orange slice from her beer and set it on her napkin.

"I agree, but what are you going to do until then? You aren't going to stay at your place tonight, are you?"

"No," she replied, worrying the hard wooden table with her thumb. "I don't think I could get any sleep. Assuming your team is finished when we're done here, I'll head back and pack a bag. I'll get a room in the hotel next to the office in New Jersey tonight. That way I can be there first thing in the morning. I think I need to tell my boss about this now. If you question Mark Minsky, it's going to come out how you found out about all this. He needs to be prepared. Call the lawyers and do whatever it is they do to prevent any liability. He's not going to be pleased."

"Why? If I understand all this correctly, it's not related to your system at all. Your discovery got the device out of his home. You did a good thing."

"Yeah." She suddenly realized she was almost finished with her beer. She should slow down since she'd be driving to New Jersey later. "I doubt he'll see it that way. Steve isn't a very understanding person. He's going to be pissed I didn't come to him earlier. I don't know what he'll think of me involving Casey."

The conversation paused as the waitress delivered their meals. Will got another beer, and Cameron switched to water. They both tucked into the food.

"I guess I was hungrier than I thought," Cameron

commented after putting away most of the plate. The fries were nice and crispy, the fish was light and fluffy, and the tartar sauce was tangy in the way she liked. She'd nearly demolished it all.

Will smiled in answer, and Cameron thought how cute he looked just then. Geez, her mind was wandering. There was too much happening too fast for her to process. It seemed almost unreal that it had only been four days since her discovery of the chip. So much had happened since then.

"You know, this case is making me feel so out of my depth."

"How's that?"

"I don't know if you noticed," he said, gesturing to his phone sitting on the table, "but I'm not a tech guy."

She smiled back, trying not to laugh at the ancient flip phone sitting across from her brand-new iPhone gleaming on the old rough wood table. The contrast was pronounced.

"I noticed."

"I don't think I realized how advanced home technology has gotten. I didn't understand a lot of what I heard in our initial interviews with the employees at Synergistic, and if you hadn't been so patient today explaining everything to me, I'm not sure I'd have been able to understand that either."

"Wow, that's the first time anyone's ever called me patient." She looked into his eyes across the table and could see a genuine frustration on his face. He seemed a very capable man and probably wasn't used to feeling out of his depth. "Look, it's not you. Only people who do this for a living understand it. And not always even then. I'm in sales. I hardly know how this stuff works. If you felt out of your depth at SE, it's because they meant for you to. Their product, outside of the proprietary software, isn't that complicated."

"Maybe, but I've let a lot of this stuff pass me by, the home automation stuff you do, the social media. I don't understand any of it."

"And look what good that did Mr. Minsky. Someone could spy on his whole life. Every move he's made. Every place he's been, everything he's done. People like new technology because it usually makes their lives easier in some way, but they don't realize how exposed it makes them. You hear Americans always talking about how many surveillance cameras they have in England and feel superior. The information you can get being in someone's digital network far surpasses anything like that, and people don't even protect themselves. Their only concern is someone getting their social security number and opening credit cards in their names. I could do more damage in an hour with the chip that was in that hub."

"Hypothetically," he said, a hint of amusement in his voice.

"Of course, hypothetically." She grinned back. "But seriously, don't let anyone make you feel ignorant about any of this stuff. No one is an expert at everything. Even geniuses like Einstein and Neil deGrasse Tyson don't know everything. I saw Neil deGrasse Tyson on *Celebrity Family Feud* once, and he was terrible. Not to mention, you looked pretty comfortable with that gun earlier. I bet you could outshoot Einstein."

That got a smile out of him. "Eight years in the Army will make anyone comfortable with a weapon, although I bet Albert would've been pretty handy on the bomb squad."

Cameron laughed out loud at that, arranging her silverware in the middle of her plate and then pushing it to the side of the table. She settled back in the booth, feeling more comfortable than she had since finding the chip in the HTH. She was beginning to think the detective might have something to do with that, or maybe it was the beer.

"You're probably right. But seriously, if anything comes up regarding this case you don't understand, you can always ask me. That is if your tech guys can't help."

"Funny you should bring that up. We're bringing in the principals from SE tomorrow afternoon. I'm going to try to get Mr. Minsky in for an interview as well. I'd love for you to sit in on the interviews. Let us know if you notice something we're missing. Our tech guys are good, but they're unfamiliar with the extent of the Home Automation applications. If you have the time, we'd surely appreciate it."

He stunned her. Cameron assumed this would be the last involvement she'd have in the case. She couldn't help but admit to herself she was intrigued. She was curious about who had planted the device, and what they were using it for. She didn't even hesitate. She knew accepting his invitation was the only way she was going to get answers.

"Sure, happy to, but I need to talk to my boss in the

morning. I can't put it off any longer."

"Understood. Just come to the precinct when you're done. We had to schedule everything with their lawyers, so we're not starting until at least one. I'd be surprised if any of those people show up on time."

"I can do that."

"Then come on," he said, throwing enough cash on the table to cover their meal and a nice tip. "I'll walk you back to your place and wait for you to pack a bag."

The crime scene team was finished when they got to her apartment, and she quickly gathered her things. Being on the road for work so often made her a very efficient packer. She had double of all her toiletries and always kept them loaded up and ready to go, so she only needed to throw some clothes in her bag, and she was on her way. She was starting to believe Detective Will Justus was a gentleman when he carried her suitcase down to the garage for her and loaded it into her car.

The drive to New Jersey didn't take long at that time of night, and it gave her plenty of time to reflect. So much had happened this week, and it was only Wednesday. She wanted to research more on Synergistic tonight, see what she was getting into tomorrow. She needed to reach out to the guys on her team, find out about the service for Casey, but she didn't want to dwell on that or the possibility that she contributed to it. Until she heard from the detectives, denial seemed like the best option. It was the only way she could keep it together. She could compartmentalize. Working for SmartTech had taught her to set emotion aside and focus on the task in front of her.

Sleep was elusive that night. She tossed and turned, running through all her actions since the previous Friday. What, if anything, she could've done differently? Dreading her meeting tomorrow. No matter what happened, she was sure Steve was going to be pissed off.

Freakin' Steve.

CHAPTER TWENTY-FIVE

ANOTHER UNCOMFORTABLE CHAIR, ANOTHER GRUMPY OLD MAN

CAMERON was sitting in another uncomfortable chair, staring at a clock on the wall, and having a strange sense of déjà vu during her meeting with Steve. To say it hadn't been going well was an understatement. He was on a call when she knocked on the open door to his office first thing Wednesday morning. He'd looked irritated when he saw who it was and waved her in to wait. And boy, did he make her wait. It was a little game he played, his way of saying "My time is more important than yours." Such a petty move, but she was a little grateful for his pettiness that day. She spent her time waiting for his call to end by trying to get her thoughts together. Trying to map out a way to explain the situation that wouldn't piss him off. No matter what she came up with, she hadn't figured it out yet.

When he finally got around to dealing with her and she

began her story, his expression slowly morphed from a mask of irritation into one of pure anger. She could tell he wanted to lay into her, but he held it back. He didn't say a word after she completed her recounting of the events of the past week. He just put the phone on his desk on speaker and asked his secretary to call up the heads of HR and the legal department ASAP. Then he sent her outside to wait.

She'd been sitting outside his office in the uncomfortable chair against the wall in awkward silence with Abby Maria for over an hour. She'd heard raised voices coming from the office but couldn't make anything out. She was playing a game with herself, trying to decide how much longer she would wait before she just got up and walked out, even though she knew she never would. There were a lot of challenges in her job, but deep down she loved it. As tough and high-stress as it was, she was surrounded by exceptionally smart people who were all extremely hardworking. She'd learned more working at SmartTech than she thought she could. Not only about sales but about teamwork and friendship as well as business. There was something magical about being in a room with so much talent, soaking it all up and finding a way to hold your own and be respected among such high-caliber people. The sense of validation was indescribable. She'd found something in SmartTech she hadn't even realized she'd been looking for. She hadn't known how much her job meant to her until she was so close to losing it.

The ring of the phone on Abby Maria's desk jolted her out of her self-reflection. Steve's assistant gave her a slight nod, indicating she should go back inside. Her look of pity was obvious. Seemed like Cameron wasn't the only one who thought this might be her last day at SmartTech.

Walking back into the office, she saw her fate clearly. Steve was seated at his large wooden desk but not facing her. His fingers steepled near his face, his attention was directed out the windows overlooking the lobby of the SmartTech complex. He could see all the SmartTech buildings from his office. King over all he surveyed. How had she never noticed how narcissistic that was until this moment? The lawyer was seated at the conference table to the side, also taking care not to look her in the eye. The only person to meet her gaze was Sandy, the HR rep. And it was never good to have the attention of HR.

"Please sit, Ms. Caldwell," Sandy said from her position leaning against the front of Steve's desk, putting herself uncomfortably close to the chair she gestured for Cameron to use. Sandy waited for her to sit before she continued. "Steve, Chris, and I have just been discussing the events of the past few days. There are some things we need you to clear up for us." She paused in her speech, waiting for some sort of response so Cameron gave her a nod. "Did you ask Casey Keane to examine an HTH you received from one of your customers on Monday?"

"Yes," she answered hesitantly.

"You are aware of SmartTech's policy on not troubleshooting or offering tech support for third-party devices, correct?"

"Yes." This was not the direction she thought they'd be going. She thought they'd focus on Casey's death or the possible liability concerns for the company if their connection to all this got out. Why were they asking questions about tech support?

"You knowingly violated company policy. You used company resources for your own purposes. Effective immediately, you're suspended without pay."

Cameron felt her stomach drop. It was over. She finally got their line of questioning. They probably hadn't had time to investigate or examine any of the legal repercussions that might arise from either Casey's or Matt Rodriguez's cases. They probably also figured that she hadn't legally done anything wrong. But they wanted her out, and this was the way they could do it. She imagined her suspension would peter on for a while until they got around to firing her. Or until she got desperate for money and quit. That was the more likely option. Living in New York wasn't cheap, and she couldn't get by for long without getting paid. She had maybe three months of expenses in savings, but it would go quickly.

At that moment, she felt the loss in her entire body. Her heart hurt and her body got hot. All that work, five years at SmartTech, the move to NYC, the camaraderie of her team. All of it was just gone. No more Friday therapy calls with Bill and Phil. She wouldn't have stories to contribute now. And what about her clients? She loved working with them, even the crazy ones like Barry. It was all just over. The worst part was, no matter how she tried to justify what happened, it was unmistakably her fault. She'd made the decisions that led her here and had no one to blame but herself.

She must have been sitting in that dreadful silence for too long because Sandy broke the quiet with a terse "You can go now."

It was enough to shock her out of her self-deprecating thoughts and get her moving to the door. She had just reached for the handle when she heard Steve's harsh "Wait."

"Steve—" Chris tried to interject to silence whatever was coming, but he was stopped from continuing with a sharp hand movement.

"You went rogue. You violated company policy, and you dragged one of our best people into your crap with you. The repercussions of this will be enormous. I just want you to know, whatever is said here, whatever happens, I hold you personally responsible for all of it."

With that parting shot, Steve killed her career with the same efficiency he ran his business.

Cameron made a vow to herself. She may have brought Casey into this, but she wouldn't give up until it was finished and the person responsible for his death was punished.

CHAPTER TWENTY-SIX

JUST A SALESGIRL

BRIGHT and early Wednesday morning, Will, Alan, Captain Lovett, and ADA Goodrich were back in the conference room, updating their board and discussing the case. The captain was pleased with their progress. They finally had a direction to take the investigation. The ADA had joined them, as Kim wanted to be present during the interrogations. She was concerned regarding the admissibility of the technical evidence and wanted to be on hand to make sure the investigation was all done by the book. She wasn't hiding her irritation at the suggestion of Cameron Caldwell's continuing association with the case, a sentiment Alan seemed to share.

"Doug and the tech team were able to confirm Ms. Caldwell's story regarding the HTH and the chip she found. It is a transmitter. It records and sends every bit of data connected to the network," Alan reported. "No audio capabilities when it's not connected to the HomeTech Hub, so at least they don't have to worry what they say around it. They're unable to determine where the data is being sent except it's to a cloud account of some sort. They tell me trace is next to impossible, but they'll keep trying."

"Was it able to transmit last night?" the captain questioned.

"It was, so we can assume whoever controls this thing now knows we have it."

"We can't use it," Kim broke in. "There's no chain of custody. We can't prove where it came from or apparently who it belongs to. We only have the girl's word that it was found in Mr. Minsky's home."

Will felt a sense of agitation at her words. *The girl.* Typical Kim, passive-aggressively undermining Cameron even though she wasn't present. Her negativity wasn't helpful. "That may be true, but at least we have a new line of questioning to pursue. We have Mr. Minsky coming in today. We'll know then if he was aware of the device and if he has any suspicion as to who would've planted it."

"Good," said the captain. "Maybe he can point us in a new direction. Have we narrowed down the suspect pool at all?"

"It has to be someone from SE," Alan answered. "We've checked out his life completely. He was a workaholic. We can't find any associations he had outside of work. No outstanding debts, no girlfriend minus his 'indiscretions' with Tessa Wells, he didn't drink, gamble, or do drugs. The more we look at this, the more convinced I am his murder has something to do with Synergistic. And Synergistic is the HomeTech Hub."

"And we've ruled out a random attack?" the captain asked.

"It was too complex. Getting into that facility with a hacked security card took planning. Random is out," Alan replied.

"We got the medical examiner's report back," Will added. "Time of death somewhere between eight and midnight last Friday, as we assumed. Three blows to the head. No trace that helps us. No security footage, and it doesn't help that most SE employees were at the CEO's house in the Hamptons that night. They all alibi each other out. It's at least a two-hour drive to his place in Southampton. It's hard to believe any of the three people we're interviewing today could've gone unnoticed for four hours. They even had a big toast at eleven that night, and we can confirm through multiple sources and with pictures that they were all there for that."

"It's only half an hour by helicopter," Kim stated.

"What?" the captain said.

"Helicopter," she said again like they were slow. "It's how I travel when I go to the Hamptons. It's much quicker, and you can avoid all the traffic. There are helicopter pads all over from Southampton to Montauk. A lot of people even have one at their house."

"I imagine someone would've noticed a helicopter taking off and landing during the party," Alan commented. Will recognizing his shock that it would be Kim who contributed logistics to their case as he shared the sentiment. Although, he supposed, being a bitch didn't mean she wasn't a smart bitch.

"It could be done," Will added thoughtfully. "They could've taken off and landed from a neighbor's house, somewhere far enough away not to be conspicuous. And there's plenty of places to land in the city. Let's find out if any of that group have a helicopter or can fly one. Landing a helicopter in the city has to leave a trail."

"They could've hired someone to fly them," Kim stated. "There are also charter flights you can take. They run on a schedule. Sort of like a taxi for the wealthy."

"Good call. Let's run it all down. See if it would be possible for any of them to have made the trip. Have we considered the possibility of a contract killing?" The captain asked.

"We did," Will answered. "We can't get a warrant for the financials to check, but it doesn't feel right. The murder was sloppy. The only thing that was professional about it was the technical part. They were efficient in wiping the security footage as well as the victim's complete technical footprint. They got all his work. That only reinforces the idea that this murder is about the company and most likely committed by someone there. A professional killer would've been a lot less messy. And with their level of security, it would take someone with the familiarity of the company to get into the server room and delete all his hard drives. While it's possible they could've given someone instructions to do it, it's unlikely."

"Agreed. What about the family?"

This time Alan replied. "They're in town. We've given them leave to collect the victim's personal effects from both the office and his apartment. CSI teams have already been through everything. They don't know anything. Hadn't seen the victim in months. Although they will receive a substantial inheritance, they all have alibis. We can confirm they were all in Texas. One thing was odd. We didn't find a HomeTech Hub in the victim's apartment. Either he didn't have one, which I find hard to believe, or someone removed it. Maybe someone was spying on him as well."

"Good work. Looks like we've got some solid leads. But we have zero evidence. Please use your interrogation time today wisely to find us some. I'm sure the ADA would appreciate it." The captain stood and nodded at Kim. "Now if there's nothing else, I'll let you get to it."

"One more thing, Captain," Will said. "I've asked Cameron Caldwell to listen in on the interviews today."

"You can't be serious, Will," Kim said. "We don't need some salesgirl in here messing things up."

Will ignored her, only looking at the captain. "If this case all ties back to the HomeTech Hubs, then we're all a little out of our depth. None of us know much about it except for Alan playing *Jeopardy!* with it."

"I ripped that thing out as soon as I got home last night," Alan added. "I can't shake the feeling that it's spying on me now."

"My point being she might notice something we don't. Or can tell us if they're lying about any of the technical points."

The captain seemed thoughtful while Kim piped up again. "This is ridiculous. We have our tech people for this kind of thing. Bring in Doug Pernick."

"I've talked to Doug about this as well. This isn't his area of expertise. He agreed with me."

"Okay," the captain agreed. "She can listen in behind the wall. She can't be directly involved in the interrogation. And, Will, she's your responsibility."

"Understood, sir."

"So, what? Is she hot? Can't get a date another way so you've got to use work to get laid? So lame, Will," Kim said, venom in her voice.

Will didn't reply, knowing to engage a dialogue with Kim like that would just encourage her. She reminded him of some of the girls he knew in high school. So well behaved in front of the teachers, but when the adult's back was turned, their true colors showed. She was also highly competitive with other women. He assumed that was what was going on here. She had no reason to oppose Cameron's involvement. She just liked always being the smartest person in the room, so having Cameron around would certainly ruffle her feathers.

CHAPTER TWENTY-SEVEN

LEGANO… ILLEGANO… IS GRAY AREA.

WHEN Cameron walked into the conference room, she felt the tension in the air. It was on the small side, shabby on the surface. It looked pretty much like any other conference room she'd ever been in, but something about it felt different. Like the cop vibes had a presence.

She'd arrived at the precinct a little before noon. The officer who'd shown her up to the conference room had been polite and courteous, perhaps sensing her nervousness. Something about being in a police station made her feel like she was in trouble, like being sent to the principal's office or like her awful morning in Steve's office. Her uneasy feeling grew when Detective Jones stood up to greet her. The look on his face was not entirely welcoming.

"Ms. Caldwell, thanks for coming in today. Can we get you some coffee?" he asked, leading her to a seat at the table in the middle of the room. At least this chair was a standard rolling desk chair with a little padding. It was a step up from the metal one they'd had her use in the interrogation room.

"No, thank you. I've already reached my caffeine limit for the day." She felt like she was crawling out of her skin.

The table was covered in files, and as she turned to sit, she got her first look at the murder board on the wall. She felt something in her heart shift as she noticed Casey's picture on the board. Instead of sitting down as she'd planned to, she walked up to begin studying the information there. Casey's cheesy work headshot looked so out of place on that board. So empty, completely devoid of his infectious personality. He was dressed in a sport coat for the picture, and it made him look like a little kid dressing up in his father's clothes.

She continued her perusal and saw a picture of the three principals at SE, who she'd researched the night before. Trey Howell and his two best friends, Tessa Wells and Brandon Reece. There were timelines and notes under each picture. Most disturbing were the crime scene photos of Matt Rodriguez. It was so shocking she had to look away for a minute and catch her breath. She worried for a second that her coffee may come back up.

As she took a few deep breaths to steady herself, she caught Alan watching her. Well, so what if he was judging? She'd never seen a dead body before and was glad these were just pictures. She couldn't imagine seeing a human being destroyed like that in person. It was almost too much as it was.

"You know Detective Justus, and this is ADA Kim Goodrich. She'll be prosecuting this case," Detective

Jones added.

Will nodded at her, not rising from his seat, barely glancing up from the papers in front of him. His change in attitude from the night before was evident. She couldn't tell if he was more withdrawn from her or just focused.

"I'll be prosecuting this case if you can manage to find me a suspect. And preferably some evidence," the ADA replied snidely. Her pinched face had an air of malice in it. "We're so glad you're here, Ms. Caldwell. I can't wait to hear a salesperson's insights into a murder case. I'm sure you'll have all this wrapped up in no time."

Detective Jones sighed, appearing resigned, and Will looked up to glare at Kim after her short comments. But both seemed accustomed to the ADA's poor attitude, so Cameron tried not to take it personally. She'd met people like Kim before and knew confrontation rarely helped things, but she couldn't seem to help herself.

"No problem. I'm happy to be here. I know I'm not a detective, but I have watched a lot of *Law and Order*, so I'm feeling pretty confident about this," she replied with a straight face, now feeling completely out of place but unwilling to let the bitchy ADA push her around. She expected a little more support from Will after the break-in last night and how kind he had been to her at dinner, but she guessed things were different in the office than out of it. "What is it you want me to do exactly?"

"We have Mike Minsky and Trey Howell coming in for interviews today. We'd like you to listen in on the interviews and make note of any technical discrepancies you notice. Ms. Wells and Mr. Reece had an obligation in San Francisco they couldn't miss, so we'll be talking to them again tomorrow. Will you be able to join us then as well, or do you need to get back to work?" Will asked.

"Work won't be a problem. I can be here tomorrow too if you think it'll be helpful."

"Meeting with your boss didn't go well today?" he asked, finally meeting her eyes.

"Let's just say I've got plenty of free time for the foreseeable future."

"Did they fire you?" the ADA asked. Then, reacting to the disapproving glares of the detectives at her bluntness, she added, "What? I need to know from a legal standpoint if her being here has any conflicts that may hinder our prosecution."

"Technically, I'm on suspension. But since that has never happened to anyone before, I imagine I'll be fired as soon as my boss has more time to consult with our lawyers and HR regarding the liability he may face from my dismissal. It's just a matter of time."

"I'm sorry," Will said.

"No worries," she answered, pasting on a smile. "I'll find something else. But to your concerns regarding your legal position, neither I nor SmartTech have done anything illegal to this point regarding your investigation." *Or anything that I'll ever admit to, anyway.* "I was given Mr. Minsky's HomeTech Hub from his representative to test, as we do all the time for our customers. There's a long precedent for it. You'll find nothing out of line there."

That seemed to satisfy the ADA, and she nodded.

"The first one in today will be Mike Minsky. What do we know about him?" Kim asked the room.

Alan answered. "He's been friends with Trey Howell since they were kids. They were roommates for a time at a boarding school up near Boston. Look to still be good friends, and he was one of the primary investors in SE. He put up the money for Trey to start the business when they were in college and Trey's dad had cut him off. He's still heavily involved with the company and good friends with all our suspects and the victim. We found pictures of the five of them together all over *Page Six*."

"Too bad we don't know specifically what was connected to his system, which devices they were spying on. Maybe then we'd have a better idea of what they were looking for," Kim said wistfully.

"Um…." Cameron paused before finishing her sentence. "I can tell you that."

"Oh God, I knew it," Kim said, looking up toward the sky, her face still holding that pinched expression. "How'd you get that information? It was illegal, wasn't it?"

"Not exactly. SmartTech was asked to troubleshoot problems with the control system, which includes anything connected to it. As an employee, I technically had permission to scan his system."

"Technically?" Alan asked.

"Legally," Cameron insisted, not about to tell them about her breaking in and taking his hard drives. Hopefully, it'd be a while before anyone would miss them. And she was sure the police would do a search of the property, adding more suspects if the theft was discovered. "It's legal. I just didn't tell anyone I did it. Casey died and I was suspended before I got the chance."

Will shuffled back in his seat, looking at her with a little more interest than he had before. Glancing up, he rolled his eyes as the ADA got up to pace. "When did you do this?"

"Right after I got the customer information from Digital Lifestyles and Casey and I found out what the chip could do. I had the same thought. Before we brought our information to anyone, Casey and I wanted to know exactly what someone was using the device for."

"All right, lay it out for us," Kim demanded, her back turned to them. Her slim frame made her look fragile, in stark contrast to her sharp attitude.

"I'm afraid it won't be very much help," Cameron said, reaching into her messenger bag for her iPad. "Do you guys have email so I can send this list to you?"

All three of them dug for business cards and handed them over. Cameron sent the info to each of them. She was a little surprised Detective Justus even had email, and he must have read that on her face as she took his card.

"What? I have email. I'm not completely in the dark ages" he said, not looking at all offended. "Why do you say this won't help?"

"Because this guy is seriously into technology," she replied. She'd logged into the station's network using the password carelessly posted on the wall like in most offices and then connected via AirPlay to the TV in the room. Will startled a bit when he watched the TV come on and the list appear on the screen. She smiled at him. "As you can see, he has everything. Smart locks, shades, two laptops and a desktop computer, two tablets, three smartphones, surveillance cameras, smartwatch, fitness tracker, smart TVs, streaming audio, smart HVAC, and his smart home gear. He even has a smart refrigerator. And that's just the regularly attached items. There are another hundred or so visiting devices. With all the data the hub was collecting, you could tell anything about this guy, and most of his friends."

"What the hell are visiting devices?" Will asked, rubbing between his eyes like he had a headache.

"Anybody who went to his home and joined his Wi-Fi with their phone, tablet, laptop, whatever. Say he had a party and other people jumped on his network. The HTH would be able to access their data as well. And that includes stored passwords and information to all the places they had been as well."

"Give us an example," Alan said. "Say it's a personal thing. We had some information that he's in the process of separating from his wife. Heading to divorce. Is this something an angry ex could use in a divorce case? Or to gather information for blackmail of some sort?"

"Absolutely. You'd be able to tell everywhere he went via his smartphone info. Presuming he has the location setting turned on, and most people do by default, it would track him wherever he went. Pairing that with the fitness tracker, you'd always have his location even if he didn't take his phone. Good info to have. Even better, you'd have full access to all information on his phones, computers, and tablets. Text messages, voice mails, any photos sent. You could also tap into his surveillance cameras. He didn't have any inside the main house, but he does have them around the perimeter and in the pool area. If he was cheating there, you'd have proof. He also has a video doorbell. You'd have pictures of anyone who came and went and when. Very lucrative divorce info."

"It'd be legal too. If she's the wife, it's technically her house too. She'd have legal rights to any of that technology," Kim said.

"Casey and I…." She paused, blinking back her welling tears. It was hard to talk about him. "Casey and I thought of this and discarded it. Mr. Minsky isn't very concerned with hiding his indiscretions. We found a ton of pictures of him with other women all over the web. We didn't have to look very hard. Seems a bit redundant for the wife to be behind this. She doesn't need the ammunition,"

Alan seemed thoughtful. "Okay, and if it's a business thing? Give me an example."

"That's a little more theoretical," Cameron said thoughtfully. "I've been giving it some thought, and I can tell you what I'd do. Mr. Minsky works at a bank, right?" They nodded. "So, if he goes to work and takes his iPad and his laptop, and he logs into the wireless network there that's secured, then when he goes home at night and the devices connect to the HTH, it would pass along his saved password information and most of the authentication you'd need to get into their system. It wouldn't take much for someone skilled in technology to hack into that bank and do anything they wanted."

"Holy shit," Will breathed. "We could be looking at a bank robbery or securities fraud? This could be about corporate espionage?"

"It could be," she confirmed. "But it gets even worse. It would do the same thing with any network he connected to. Most corporations have guest networks, like you do here, for visitors to log into. They keep all their sensitive stuff on another network only for employees. But not all of them do, and even if they do, sometimes people will put you on the regular network anyway. They tend to be faster and allow for better presentations. Happens to me all the time." Kim was nodding along; it tracked that she'd be able to relate to this part. "Think about this. Mr. Minsky goes to meet a customer. By all accounts, his customers are large Fortune 500 companies. He has his iPad at their office, using the wireless access given to him while he was there. The same thing would happen. When he got home, that info would be transmitted as well."

"Shit," Will said again. "You're right. It doesn't narrow it down much."

"The only thing we found in the chip's software design that might help is there's a setting in the code to determine which device information takes priority over another. That's why Casey and I focused on this being something directed either at the bank or insider trading. Priority was given to Minsky's computers over his personal tech."

She was explaining the details of the code and its implications when the door to the conference room opened and a uniformed officer poked his head in.

"Excuse me, sir," he said, looking at Will. "Mr. Minsky is here. We have him in interview room one."

"Thanks, Nick," he replied. "Well," he said, addressing the room, "let's see if Mr. Minsky can narrow this down for us."

CHAPTER TWENTY-EIGHT

MEETING THE MYSTERIOUS MR. MINSKY

WILL installed Kim and Cameron in the room adjoining the interview room before going in to meet Mr. Minsky. To Cameron's surprise, it was almost exactly like what she had seen on cop shows. A small narrow gray room with a large two-way mirror showing the interrogation room. She felt absurdly cool to be allowed on this side of the mirror.

The excitement of the moment—or maybe her caffeine buzz—must have shown on her face because the ADA was quick to comment.

"It's only an interrogation room, not Bergdorf's."

Don't engage. Don't engage.

Cameron just rolled her eyes and focused on the activity in the room before her. She noticed it was the same one they'd put her in a few days before. Or maybe they all just looked the same.

"Mr. Minsky," Will greeted as he walked into the

conference room, "thank you for meeting with us today. I'm Detective Will Justus, and this is my partner, Detective Alan Jones."

Will and Alan both sat in chairs at the small table in the interrogation room.

"Call me Mark," he answered. "The officer who called said this was about Matt's death? I'm happy to help in any way I can."

"We appreciate that," Alan said, his manner light and friendly. "We were wondering if you can tell us how you knew Mr. Rodriguez?"

"Sure. I met Matt through my friend Trey I guess five or six years ago now. When he went to work for him."

"Your friend Trey Howell?"

"Yes, he owns Synergic Engineering, where Matt worked. When Matt joined the company, he started hanging out with us. Going to ball games, dinner, bars, that sort of thing."

"And by us you mean…?" Alan asked.

"Well, me, Trey, Tessa Wells, and Brandon Reece. We've all been friends forever, and Matt just fit right in."

"Any issues or problems between any of you?"

"No, not at all. We all get along well."

"Do you know what Matt did for SE?"

"Sure, he invented the HomeTech Hub," he said, smiling. "The guy was a genius. That thing made them all a fortune."

"And you too, right?" Will interjected. It wasn't hard to see who was playing bad cop in this interview. "You're an investor in the company. You made a lot of money as well."

Kim commented, "He's got to expand the line of questioning. Making money doesn't make you a murderer."

"Sure, but there are only a few motives for murder. And money, sex, and revenge top the list." She caught the ADA's skeptical glance before turning back to face the interview. "I told you, I watch a lot of *Law and Order*."

"True," Mark answered. "I invested in Trey when he first started the business. And again when I saw the prototype for the HTH. Technology is the future. And I saw the potential in the hub the first time I saw it."

"The potential for it as a consumer electronic device or as a method of data collection?" Alan asked, clearly testing the waters.

"Well, both really," Mark replied. "It's no secret that's how companies like Google make the majority of their money. The sale of collected data would fund the research at Synergistic indefinitely. The goal of the HomeTech Hub was to be as successful to marketing companies as well. The revenue of the hardware is small change compared to what it can generate long term."

"What kind of data?"

"Oh, you know, the kind of products people buy from it, who in the house uses it most. Things marketing companies can use to narrow their demographic."

"I see," Alan replied.

"This is procedure, Mr. Minsky, but can you tell us where you were last Friday night?" Will interrupted.

"Sure, I was at Trey's house in Southampton. All of SE was there celebrating the ten-million-unit mark. Matt was supposed to be there too, but he never showed."

"I see," Alan said. "And you own one of those ten million HomeTech Hubs?"

"Of course. I have several at both my houses."

"Where did you purchase these hubs?"

"I didn't," he answered. "They were gifts. Matt gave them to me."

"I see." He nodded and looked to Will, who took the cue and broke the bad news.

"Mr. Minsky, you employ a company called Digital Lifestyles for the smart home technology in your Hamptons home, is that correct?"

"Yes," he confirmed. A look of confusion formed on his face, looking unsure as to where they were taking the line of questioning.

"And you're aware there have been some issues regarding the communication between your HomeTech Hubs and the SmartTech control system?"

"Yes, I gave both Hubs that Matt gave me to the owner of Digital Lifestyles last week. He was going to have SmartTech look at them, try to see what the problem was. What does this have to do with the murder?"

"SmartTech did look at your hubs, Mr. Minsky. They found an extra chip in one of the units. We had our techs check it out and determine it's a transmitter. Someone has been spying on you, sir."

Mark went white. There was no faking the surprise on his face. "What? Jesus, for how long? What did they get?"

"We're looking into all that, Mr. Minsky. First thing,

we'd like your permission to send a technician back to your apartment in the city with you. We'd like to check your HomeTech Hub there and see if it contains the same spyware."

"Yes, of course. Christ, I can't believe this."

"Mr. Minsky, do you have any idea who would want to do this to you?" Alan asked.

"Mark, please," he replied offhandedly, getting up and beginning to pace in the small room. "First guess, I'd say my wife. We're separated. But she's not technical enough to pull something like this off. She can't even check her voice mail."

"She could've hired a PI," Will suggested. "At the advice of an attorney perhaps?"

"She doesn't have an attorney. We've been separated for over two years. She spends most of her time in Europe. Italy mainly, the south of France sometimes. I haven't seen her for at least a year. I can't see how this would benefit her unless it was simply stalking, and I wouldn't put that past her. She's in a better position now than if we divorce. We have an ironclad prenup. She wouldn't get much. Financially she's much better off staying married to me."

"Then why haven't you divorced her?" Will asked the next logical question.

Mike shrugged, still pacing. "No reason to, I guess. It's kind of an 'out of sight, out of mind' thing. And in my position, the illusion of a family man sits better with the board in some instances than a single man does. Regardless if it's just an illusion."

"You said Mr. Rodriguez gave you the hubs. Could he have done this?" Alan inquired.

"Technically I'm sure he could. But I can't see why he'd do it. We were friends. Good friends. And I was an investor in his work. I see no reason for it to be him. What could he possibly gain?"

"What about a list of people who have been to your house in Southampton while this thing has been installed? Could you give us that?"

"I wouldn't even know where to start. I have parties out there all the time, not to mention the staff. There could've been hundreds of people in that house. And I doubt I knew half of them."

They finished questioning Mr. Minsky soon after and arranged for Doug Pernick to accompany him home to inspect his HTH. They reconnected with Cameron and Kim back in the conference room.

"Anything?" Will asked them.

"I'm hopeful the unit in the city has a chip in it as well. Then we'll be able to use it during prosecution if we need to. It won't have a broken chain of custody like the last one," Kim said, looking pointedly at Cameron, who just met her gaze but said nothing, again choosing not to engage.

Be the bigger person, she chanted to herself like a mantra.

Will nodded. "Cameron?"

"I'm interested to see if there's a device in his NYC home as well," she replied. "As you know, Casey checked several other defective units at SmartTech and didn't find any other chips. If he has another one, it'll confirm this was targeted to him specifically. I also found it interesting that he said Matt gave him the hubs. He looked surprised, but what if he'd discovered them? Wouldn't that give him a motive?"

Will nodded, agreeing with them both. "Let's see what Doug finds. But in the meantime, we'll look a little deeper into Mr. Minsky. And track down his wife."

"I'll start on that," Alan said, adding notes to the board under Mark Minsky's picture. "Take Kim in with you when you talk to Trey Howell. I have a feeling with his lawyer in the room, it might be a different type of interview."

Alan was right, Cameron thought as she watched Will sitting in the interview room with Kim by his side. Cameron was again watching through the two-way mirror, this time alone. The room seemed a little lighter without Kim's presence, and Cameron felt like she could breathe a little easier. Trey Howells's attorney had been contentious since they'd started, barely letting his client answer any of their questions. It was the second time they had met, and it didn't seem like Will's opinion of Trey Howell had improved. He was trying to sell the aw-shucks, good-ole-boy persona just a little too hard, and Will didn't seem to be buying it.

Cameron could also see the shark behind the shiny veneer. If her experience in sales had taught her anything at all, it was how to read people, and she didn't like what she saw in Trey Howell. But what was he hiding? The motive for murder, covering for a friend? Or was he just protecting his business? It was impossible to tell at this point and would continue to be unless Will could get some straight answers out of him.

"Mr. Howell, I understand your feelings about having an attorney present, but please keep in mind you haven't been charged with a crime. We're simply trying to get more information and discover why someone would want to kill your friend. Can you please help us?"

Trey Howell looked to his lawyer, who gave him a single nod.

Maybe now they would get somewhere.

CHAPTER TWENTY-NINE

SCAN, DISCARD, SELECT, MOVE ON

THE two detectives, one lawyer, and the suspended sales manager reconvened in the conference room after the interview. It was almost the start of a bad joke.

"We learned nothing," Will stated. Frustrated, he sprawled out in a chair at the table, wiping his face with his hands. "We're nowhere closer on this than we were yesterday."

"I talked to Minsky's wife. She is indeed in Europe. Been living in Greece for the last six months. Hasn't talked to her husband. Doesn't care. I think we can take her off the suspect list." Alan added.

"Again, nowhere."

"I don't know about that. She said if we were looking into her husband, we should look at Tessa Wells. The wife claims they'd been having an affair through the whole marriage. Said they'd been sleeping together since high school. Claimed Trey and Brandon had been with her as well."

"That's interesting," Kim said. "They seem like a close group. I wonder if there's any jealousy going on there. Or maybe Tessa wanted to marry Mark and was looking for dirt to break up the marriage. Maybe the spyware was planted to spy on the wife."

"Or Matt could've done it," Will said. "He got involved with Tessa as well. Got jealous of her relationship, was trying to find a way to get between them, and one of them found out. Gives them both motives."

"These are all good theories, but we need more information. There's no evidence of anything at this point," Alan said pointedly. "We just have more questions. Will's right, we're getting nowhere."

"I don't know about that," Cameron added. "Trey Howell lied to you."

"What?" Will exclaimed, raising his head off the table to look at her. "When?"

"I don't know if it means anything, but he lied when you asked him if they had the ability to manufacture the chip. He said no, but they absolutely could."

Kim was now looking at her with a little less disdain than she had earlier in the day. "Explain."

"Well, Trey said all their manufacturing facilities are overseas. That's not true. They have a small production facility in upstate New York. It was part of a marketing scheme to get some tax write-offs and highlight them bringing back American manufacturing jobs. They opened it when they started producing the hubs. Trey did the ribbon-cutting, see?" She reconnected her iPad to the TV on the wall in the conference room and brought up the article she'd found on the internet announcing the plant. "But that's not all." She tapped on her tablet for a bit and brought up a new set of pictures. "These are photos of the SE offices here in Manhattan. A PR article Trey did when he was named one of the top ten most eligible bachelors in the city. See those machines behind him? They're 3D printers. Each one can print with different kinds of plastic. You use them to create prototypes."

She turned around to see them all looking at her quizzically.

"What?" she said. "SmartTech has some. We use them for preproduction models to test the prototypes before we pay to have them made. It saves a ton of time and money when we develop new products. And see this picture?" She pointed to a new photo. "See behind him? Those are all components to build boards and chips. I can't see everything, but those are circuit boards. There's a soldering iron. It's a workroom. They have the capability to make a chip there. Most tech companies would. I mean, some people send everything out to be made, but it's more expensive and takes a lot of time. For a company as profitable as Synergistic, it only makes sense to do it in-house. And you need to understand, building a device like this isn't the hard part. You could buy the hardware part at a million places in the city. There's nothing special about it. It's the programming, the software that would be the most complicated. And you could do that anywhere."

"Son of a bitch!" Will exclaimed, slamming the files in his hands onto the table and scattering papers everywhere. "He lied to me."

"I assume he thought you wouldn't catch it," Cameron said. "But more importantly, why did he lie? It isn't that big of a deal. It's a stupid thing to lie about. There are hundreds of facilities like that in Manhattan. Or hell, you could even make it in your apartment with the right gear. Again, the hardware portion isn't unique. Is it because he made the chip or that he knows someone at his company did and he's covering for them?"

"Son of a bitch," Will repeated, trying to corral the scattered papers. "He knows something."

"This is good, right?" Cameron questioned. "And he doesn't know you know he lied. Could be useful." She smiled at Will.

"Looks like you aren't useless after all," Kim interrupted their exchange, ruining the moment. "I have to head back to the office. Let me know when you find out about Minsky's apartment. I'd like to know if we have some admissible evidence. That way I can prepare if you guys end up needing warrants. Though how I'll explain this to a judge, I don't know."

"I could help you with that if the technology is too much for you," Cameron said sweetly, garnering her a scalding look from Kim before she turned away.

No one bothered to tell her goodbye as she made a rather dramatic exit out the door, artfully draping her scarf around her neck and throwing her coat over her shoulders. She seemed to put a little extra swing in her hips as she moved out of the room.

When Cameron looked over, she saw both detectives studiously eying the board, not even glancing at the ADA, and she wondered if the woman knew that little show had only been for her benefit.

CHAPTER THIRTY

THE HYPOTHETICAL POINT AT WHICH TECHNOLOGICAL GROWTH BECOMES UNCONTROLLABLE AND IRREVERSIBLE

"CAM," Will said emphatically.

"Huh?" she said, snapping herself out of her thoughts. She must not have heard him the first time he called to her.

"Can you stay?" he asked. "I'd like you to be here when we brief the captain. I'd also like to have you coordinate with Doug about whatever he finds at the Minsky house. Are you up for it? We can order some food."

"Sure," she agreed. "It's not like I have anything else to do."

His face fell at her comment. "I'm sorry you lost your job over this."

"It's not your fault. And who knows? Right now I'm just suspended. Maybe I won't get fired," she said, putting on a brave face even though they both knew the truth. Her job was history.

Cameron, Will, and Alan fell into a comfortable rhythm after that. It was almost like working with Bill and Phil. It seemed the underlying tension in the room disappeared with the ADA's departure. Cameron started to wonder if there was more to her lack of hospitality than just an unusually harsh disposition. She studied Will covertly under the guise of searching for more info on her tablet. He might have had a history with the woman. Although unpleasant, she was beautiful. She could see the two of them having a fling, though it was hard to imagine them together long term with their obvious personality differences. She was an uptight elitist, and he had a down-to-earth easygoing nature. But stranger things had happened. And they did say opposites attracted.

He caught her looking at him and smiled. His attitude toward her had certainly changed since she'd arrived that morning. She had to wonder how much of that was directly related to the absence of Kim. But it could just be his nature. She'd only known him for two days. She told herself it was foolish to make assumptions about his character.

They ordered in a ton of Chinese food around five, and it was delivered right before the captain walked in.

"Looks like I'm right on time as always," he joked, joining them at the conference table. He stuck his hand out for Cameron to shake. "I'm Gil Lovett. You must be Ms. Caldwell "

"Cameron," she said, grinning. She immediately liked the man. "Nice to meet you."

"And you as well. I'd like to thank you for coming forward with the information you had. Most people would've buried it. I heard it cost you your job. I'm sorry about that, and I'm sorry about your friend. It's a damn shame."

"Thank you," she said as she took a deep breath to steady herself from the emotions starting to well up. She'd been able to put it out of her mind all day while working with the police. The guilt and loss were too overwhelming to dwell on. She took another breath. "I appreciate that. And I appreciate you letting me help. It feels good to be able to contribute to catching whoever did this. I think that'll help, when they're finally put away."

The captain held her gaze and nodded once sincerely. She knew then that he understood how she was feeling and would be as accommodating as he could be.

"Now, catch me up. Where are we?"

They took him through what they had learned during the interviews.

"Doug also discovered an identical chip in Mr. Minsky's apartment in the city," Will told him. "It looks like he was the only target."

"What's the motive?" the captain asked. "I can't see the benefit. Is it financial gain? If so, how? Is it personal?"

"We don't know," Alan answered.

"I think the best way to look at it is by who could've done it," Cameron said, then walked to the murder board and flipped it to the other side. She picked up a dry-erase marker and wrote three names at the top of the board: Trey Howell, Matt Rodriguez, and Tessa Wells. "These three people are the most likely suspects as to who made the chip. They have the technical knowledge and access to Minsky's hubs. Once we figure that out, we'll have a better idea of the motive for this whole thing. I also think the absence of an HTH in Matt's apartment is important. My guess is whoever planted the chip on Mark Minsky did the same thing to Matt. He found out, and that's why he was killed. Which, if true, would rule him out as the doer."

"I get Howell and Rodriguez, but Tessa Wells? Does she have the technical knowledge to do this?" the captain asked.

"She does," Cameron answered. "She may have her MBA and be running sales at SE, but I found mention of a computer science major in her undergrad work and some programming awards she won in college. Combined with the resources she had at SE, she could've done it."

"But not Minsky or Reece?"

"No, Reece is strictly a lawyer. Nothing technical in his background. And while Minsky is definitely into technology, he doesn't have the knowledge to design and build something like this. He's a user, not a maker. He'd have to contract it out, and that would be noticed."

"Hmmm, interesting way to look at it. But all your suspects have alibis. They were all at the party together."

"They were," confirmed Will. "But Kim's suggestion was spot-on. They all have access to the SE helicopter. We're also running the charter manifests from the companies who provide service to the Hamptons to see if anyone used that to travel. The timing's tight, but one of them could've snuck out, went back to the city, and committed the murder before returning to the party for the toast at eleven. We're also checking social media for pictures taken the night of the party to see if we can't exclude some of them."

"Good work. Looks like you're making some progress. How'd it go with the ADA? Any trouble there?"

"No," Will replied. "She was pleased that we found another chip but didn't add anything significant."

"What's your next step?"

"We've got interviews with Wells and Reece tomorrow. In light of what Minsky's wife said, it may open up some more avenues as we search for a motive. It seems Ms. Wells has had intimate relationships with all our suspects."

The captain's eyebrows rose at this. "All of them? Well, that is interesting. What about the car crash in New Jersey? Have the Bergen County police found any leads?"

"Not yet," replied Alan, glancing at Cameron. "They've confirmed foul play and are looking at suspects now. I've worked with the detective in charge before, and he's agreed to keep me posted if they bring anybody in."

Cameron paused eating her Szechuan chicken at that. So, it was confirmed. Casey was murdered. Deep down, she knew it wasn't an accident, but hearing it out loud was different somehow. She couldn't help but blame herself. She'd gotten him involved in all of this in the first place. She could've just ignored it. Put the chip back where she'd found it. If she had, Casey would still be alive, and she would still have a job.

She shook herself out of that train of thought. Looking back didn't do any good. She couldn't change what had happened, but she could help catch his killer, and maybe with a little luck and by keeping SmartTech out of this whole affair, she could manage to get her job back as well.

After giving herself her little pep talk, she pushed her food away; she wasn't hungry anymore. She looked up to see Detective Justus looking at her thoughtfully.

"It's late, guys. Maybe it's time we call it a night," he said.

"Agreed," said the captain. "Good work today. Keep me posted after your interviews tomorrow." With that, he left the room.

Cameron began packing up her equipment as well. She laughed to herself at the differences between her and Detective Justus's work bags. Hers was full of electronics. Laptop, iPad, chargers, two phones, Raspberry PI, backup batteries, flash drives, etc. Will's was all paper.

The long day was starting to take its toll, but she was dreading going back to her apartment alone. She hadn't been back since the break-in the night before, and her place was still a disaster. She'd have to clean the bedroom at least before she could get any sleep. Hopefully they hadn't trashed all her pillows.

"Are you going to stay at your apartment tonight?" Will asked.

"Yep," she replied. "I can't stay at a hotel forever. And now that everything is out in the open, no one has a reason to come after me."

He nodded. "Do you want to go grab a drink first? Then I'll take you home and check it out for you. Just to be on the safe side."

"Sounds good," she agreed, relieved. As tired as she was, she wanted to avoid the reality of her apartment for a little while longer.

"Al, you in?"

"No," he answered. "You two go ahead. I should go home and beg for forgiveness from my wife for getting rid of our HTH. I think she was starting to like AIME more than she likes me."

Cameron grinned. "I can relate. I knew I had a problem when I started thanking mine. I'd ask her to play a song for me and thank her when she did. It only made me realize how close to the singularity we are."

Alan laughed, shaking his head at her.

"What's the singularity?" Will asked.

"You'll need a drink before I even start trying to explain the singularity to you," Cameron teased.

CHAPTER THIRTY-ONE

IF YOU GO TO A BAR WITH A COP, CAN HE ARREST YOU WHEN YOU LEAVE FOR BEING DRUNK IN PUBLIC?

WILL took Cameron to a bar a few blocks away from the police station, but not the local cop bar. He didn't want them to constantly be interrupted by his coworkers, though he couldn't explain why. And it wasn't something he was looking too closely at. He also wanted to take her somewhere a little more upscale. Something like he assumed she was used to. Although she had seemed right at home in the old Irish pub last night, so maybe not. It was so hard to tell with women.

He ended up taking her to a quiet wine bar. It was classy but not pretentious, and he needed something with a little more bite than his usual beer tonight, and they had a great liquor selection as well. The lighting was dark, but there were lamps on the tables. It was a nice effect in contrast to all the dark wood. He liked the feel of it and found himself hoping she did too. They got a table near the bar, and their server was with them immediately. Cameron ordered a pinot noir, and he got a scotch.

"So," he said, "Kentucky? How'd you get from Kentucky to NYC?"

"Ah, you did your homework on me, I see."

"We did. We had to treat you just like every citizen bringing us information on a case."

"So, like a suspect?" she teased.

"Yeah, pretty much, but it didn't take us long to rule you out." He liked that she was grinning. He knew women who would've been offended at the background check, but Cameron didn't seem to be.

"So Kentucky. Um, I got here by way of California. If you want to move up in my business, you have to go where the jobs are. And as you can imagine, there's not a lot of opportunity in Kentucky in luxury smart homes. Being a woman also added a degree of difficulty. But I was fortunate. I had a job I hated in California, but it turned out to be a good stepping-stone. The funny part was I hated the job so much, I'd been interviewing for another position for a long time. They fired me while I was on my way to a job interview. Ironic, huh? Regardless, I didn't get the job, but the position was with SmartTech, and they had an opening in New York. They asked me if I'd move, and I agreed. Thirty days later, I moved here."

"Wow, that's quick."

"Yeah." She laughed. "If anyone asks you how soon you

can move across the country, don't tell them thirty days. It's a bitch."

"Unless you count my military years, I've never lived anywhere but New York."

"Do you live in the city?"

"No, I've got a place in Greenpoint."

"Cool. I've worked on some neat projects there."

"Not in my building, I assure you," he said. "Are you okay, about your job?"

That was the moment the waitress brought their drinks. Cameron took a big sip before she replied. "This helps." She grinned at the wine in her hand. "No, I'm not okay. I loved that job. I was good at it. I worked hard for it. But I'm not going to write it off just yet. I don't believe in borrowing trouble. I'll wait and see what happens and deal with it then."

"Very levelheaded of you."

"I'm trying to be. With everything that's gone on this week, it'd be easy to freak out, but that wouldn't do anyone any good. If I can stay focused on what's in front of me, everything will work out just fine. Besides, I can get a new job if I have to. I'm extremely hirable."

He grinned back at her. "I bet you are."

"What about you?" she asked. "Did you always want to be a cop?"

"Definitely not." He chuckled. "I was a mess in high school. To use a cliché, I ran with the wrong crowd. My family didn't have a lot of money, and there was no way I was going to get a scholarship to college. My dad sat me down one day and told me I was going nowhere fast, and I could continue down the path I was on and have to move out immediately after I graduated high school—if I graduated high school—or I could join the military. He thought for sure that would straighten me out. I might've been a troublemaker, but I wasn't stupid. I knew what my prospects were as an eighteen-year-old kid in New York City, and they weren't good. So, I joined up."

"And did it straighten you out?"

"Yes, ma'am." He smiled, taking a sip of his scotch. "I spent eight years in the service. When I got out, I just couldn't see myself doing anything else. I couldn't imagine working in an office nine-to-five every day. I had some friends from my unit who'd joined the force, and they seemed to like it, so it felt like the right move for me."

Their drinks were dwindling by then, and the waitress noticed without any prompting. She asked them if they wanted another round. They agreed quickly, and she was on her way.

"Do you like it?"

"Most days," he replied honestly. "Some days more than others. You can't imagine some of the things I see, but something is satisfying about putting criminals in jail. It feels like I've accomplished something at the end of the day, and I enjoy that."

"And your family? Was your dad happy to see you get all straightened out?"

"He died while I was in the service, so, unfortunately, he never got to see it. But I like to think he knows."

"I'm sorry."

"Don't worry about it." He accepted his fresh drink from the waitress. "It was a long time ago."

***

She nodded and enjoyed the quiet for a bit. She wasn't usually a fan of extended silences but sitting with Will was comfortable. They both enjoyed their drinks and the lulling piano music through the bar. It went against her better judgment, but she was starting to like the guy. It'd been a long time since Cameron had met a man she was interested in. That was the price she paid for spending eighty hours a week at her job. And she had a strict no-dating policy in her workplace. As one of the very few women in her industry, it was an edict she stood steadfastly by. She'd had one boyfriend at work before, and once was enough. It might not be fair, but there was a double standard at play. If you weren't careful, you could quickly lose the respect of your peers, and people could assume you'd slept your way to the top. It was an assumption Cameron took pains to avoid. She wanted to be judged on her merit, regardless of the effect it had on her dating life.

"I don't mean to spoil the mood, but I did have a thought regarding the case."

Will sighed but was still smiling at her. "Let's hear it."

"Why didn't the killer remove the chip for the HTH at Mike Minsky's New York apartment? They searched my place but didn't try to get the chip back from him before we could find it? It doesn't make sense."

"Good point. All right, let's go through the timeline. The killer found out the chip had been discovered when they received the transmission from the upload on Tuesday night. They immediately took action and went for Casey, but they didn't recover the chip, so they looked at your place. They found out the chip had been sent to the police from the Wednesday night transmission. The logical step would've been to go after any remaining doctored devices today after they knew we'd check."

"So that leaves only two possibilities. Either the killer assumed it was too dangerous to try to get it and not worth the risk since we already had one of them, or the killer was unable to get to the chip today."

"Tessa Wells and Brandon Reece went to San Francisco today. They wouldn't have been able to go for the chip," he said excitedly.

"Exactly," she said, reaching up with her glass to clink with his. "See, I knew watching all that *Law and Order* would pay off."

"But what's the motive? Why spy on Mark Minsky?" Will wondered out loud.

"I can think of two reasons. One, it was Tessa, and she's legitimately the most industrious stalker in the world. That would also explain why the HTH would be missing from Matt's apartment. She dated him too and was spying on him as well."

Will gave her a sideways glance before replying. "I have a hard time seeing that. What would the point be? What could she get out of it? And it seems way too advanced for some relationship drama."

"I agree, but that doesn't mean it couldn't happen. She could be trying to see if they're seeing other women, or how they felt about her or any number of things."

"Still seems farfetched. What's your second motive?"

"If it was Brandon, it's assuredly business related. He's the legal force behind the company, but both Matt and Mark were the financial backbones. Matt's product and Mark's investment. You'd have to dig to find the contract to see what percentage each one of them is getting, but I'd be willing to bet it's significant. I'd bet they were getting more than the rest of them. A lot more."

"Money's always a good motive, but even if their pay wasn't equal, Brandon can't be hurting for money. SE is raking it in. He's got to be getting a healthy chunk. And he's got family money as well. That guy is never going to be hurting for cash."

"Maybe," she agreed. "But in my business, we have a saying. 'Never sell with your own wallet.' What you think of as a 'healthy chunk' might not have been enough for Brandon. And some people, regardless of how much they have, always want more."

He nodded thoughtfully, taking a sip of his scotch and leaning back in his chair. He studied her a bit before asking his next question.

"All right, Nancy Drew, what about Trey Howell? What's his motive?"

"See, you think that's an insult, but I loved Nancy Drew." She laughed, a little warm from the wine and finding herself enjoying his company, the bar, and the conversation. It was nice to be out with a man and not have it be for work. She'd forgotten what it felt like. He was interesting and a welcome distraction from thinking about the mess she was in. Losing her job hurt, but the responsibility she felt from losing Casey hurt more.

"Okay, the motive for Trey," she said, rubbing her hands together briskly. "This one was a little harder, but I think Casey had the right idea on this one."

"Don't hold out on me now. I can't wait to hear this."

"Trey's the leader, right?" He nodded. "He is working on a whole other level than the other two. If he was behind this, it has to be a much bigger reason. Casey suggested this was a beta test. Trey would put a few chips in hubs he knew he'd have access to, to see if the data collection worked."

"Then what?"

"Then he'd sell it," she stated as if it was obvious. "Don't tell me you haven't thought about the far-reaching implications of this device? You could sell it to a foreign nation so fast your head would spin. A way to passively spy on anyone. Odds are you'd get someone important too. Government officials, business leaders, they all have a HomeTech Hub. If those chips were added to every unit in production? It would be unreal. And you wouldn't even have to do anything. People are lining up to put them in their homes."

Will didn't answer, but she could tell his mind was working overtime trying to absorb what she said. Truthfully, it was the most likely scenario. From her research, everything she read about Trey Howell showed a well-adjusted, successful businessman. He donated to charity, didn't get into trouble. But his early life was mostly blanks. She knew he'd had a falling out with his family and been cut off. Hence his need to take Mark Minsky as an investor to start SE. But he'd done well. At this point, he'd far outpaced his family fortune. From the outside, he seemed to be a man who had it all. But looks could be deceiving.

"The only issue you'd have with that would be how to store and process all the data."

"What?" Will asked.

"Well, if the data being sent every night is only from a few people, you could store it on some personal servers easily. But if it was hundreds of even the ten million people who have HomeTech Hubs now, then that would be a massive amount of data. The servers required to store it and the people required to process that amount of information would be enormous. I'm sure SE has a pretty massive server farm. I wonder if they've grown it recently?"

"Now you're taking it a little too far, edging into Tom Clancy territory. Most murders don't work like that. There's no global conspiracy. At the end of the day, it's either about money or it's about love."

After a brief argument over who would pay the bill, he won. They decided to walk from the bar back to her apartment. The New York night was clear and calm. The air was crisp with the changing of the seasons. It was Cameron's favorite time of year, before the snow came in and made the city wet, dirty, and cold, but after the summer heat when it got so hot it felt like the sun was coming up from the sidewalks and the pavement was melting. They walked slowly, enjoying the company and the city. Even though she'd only been there for five years, Cameron felt more at home in the city than she had anywhere else. There were always people around and something going on no matter the time of day or night. It fit her perfectly.

When they got to her building, Will talked with the doorman on duty. His name was Ken. Another name she could file away for future reference. After a quick conversation in which Ken assured Detective Justus he understood the situation and would keep a keen eye out, they rode the elevator up to her floor.

It took Will less than a minute to search her apartment. He met her back in the doorway and declared it safe. "Are you sure you want to stay here?" he asked, standing comfortably close to her in her small entranceway. "It's a mess."

"I'm sure," she replied softly. "I've got to deal with it sometime, and now's as good a time as any. I won't get into all of it tonight. I'll just tackle the bedroom. I've got to head to the office early in the morning. They've requested I turn in all my product samples and my computer, so… that'll be fun."

"I'm sure. Then you'll meet us at the precinct for the interviews?"

"I will."

He nodded, taking a casual glance around again at the mess before moving a step closer to her. She held her breath for a moment. The way he was looking in her eyes and the feeling seeping into her skin, she was sure he planned to kiss her. But after a beat, he stepped back.

With a quick "Be careful," he was out the door. Cameron sighed, locked the door behind him, and began the arduous task of making her apartment livable enough to sleep in.

CHAPTER THIRTY-TWO

WELL, THAT WAS AWKWARD, AND THEN IT
HURT.

DRIVING back to the city after returning her equipment
to her office, Cameron was a flood of emotions. She hated
the sympathetic looks she received from her colleagues.
Word had spread about her suspension, and though no one
mentioned it directly, she could tell what they were thinking.
But there were other looks she got, less sympathetic ones,
and she knew those people, not unlike herself, were blaming
her for what happened to Casey. While she would've usually
liked to have stayed in the office, said her goodbyes to the
people she was close to, those few who were looking at her in
less than a friendly way made her uncomfortable enough to
hurry out. All told, she spent less than thirty minutes saying
goodbye to a job she loved. She couldn't imagine how it
would be at the funeral this Saturday. As tough as she was
trying to be, she couldn't help the few tears that managed

to escape as she was leaving the SmartTech parking lot for what could be the final time.

Cameron had mostly pulled herself together during her drive. She felt composed again by the time she was preparing to make the turn from 22nd onto 2nd Avenue upon finally reaching the city. There was no left turn light there, and depending on the day, it could take seconds or many long minutes to make the turn. Some days it was the longest part of her drive.

She was planning to run up to her apartment and throw on some more comfortable clothes before heading to the police station. Now that she wasn't working, there was no need for the suit. It was habit more than anything that made her put it on that morning. Plus, she also didn't want to give anyone who might be judging her dismissal any satisfaction by going in looking like a bum.

Looking ahead to that opportunity and seeing an opening in traffic, Cameron made the turn. As soon as she did, she felt the immediate impact on her rear driver side door like she was hit by a train. The sound was deafening.

Her Jeep felt out of control, the wheel moving on its own in her hands. She was spinning and sliding down 2nd Avenue, being pushed by what looked like a big truck. Her heart raced and her throat seemed to close as she tried to scream. She couldn't quite manage to get herself to make a sound, and if she did, she couldn't hear it above the rage of screeching metal. Her hands scrambled to find purchase on the wheel as she tried to gain some control. Her car spun again, and she heard more than felt the loud crash that separated their vehicles. It looked like someone had hit the truck, ripping it away from her Jeep.

Then all of a sudden, it was quiet, and her car was stopped.

Holy shit. Holy shit.

She was moving slowly, she knew, but everything hurt, and she felt disconnected from her body. It felt like it took her hours to get her bearings, but in reality, it couldn't have been more than a minute. She reached up and felt something sticky on her forehead and wiped it away. Blood.

It's okay. Head wounds bleed.

She looked up again across her vehicle to see a man jumping down from the truck that hit her. Great. She hoped he had insurance. Her car was sure to be totaled. *But at least the airbags hadn't deployed,* she thought. *That was something.*

It took her brain a second to process that something wasn't right. The driver was wearing all black, a mask on his face, and had a gun in his hand. He wasn't getting out to help her or trade insurance info. He was trying to kill her.

Move! she told herself. *Move, move, move.*

She dove/fell across to her passenger seat when she heard the first gunshot. Almost immediately she heard the screams of the bystanders and saw people on the street take off running. She half crawled and half pulled herself out of the driver seat, trying to stay as low as possible. She opened the passenger door and slid to the pavement face-first. She caught herself with her hands and felt them scrape raw against the concrete and glass. She hid behind the front passenger side tire to get as much protection as she could while she tried to come up with a plan. She took a few deep breaths, but the shots kept coming, and she knew she wasn't safe. Who the hell fired a gun in the middle of the street in Manhattan?

Think. Think.

She needed to run. There was a police station a few blocks away. She could go that way. Surely someone had called them by now. It was her best shot.

She took a deep breath and centered herself. She checked her body. Other than her head, nothing else seemed to be hurt. Just a few scrapes on her hands. She flexed her arms and legs. Everything seemed to be in working order, if a bit sore. She was surely going to feel it in the morning.

The decision was made. It was her best option. Now she just needed to make her feet move.

Cameron grabbed her messenger bag from the passenger seat of her car, looped it over her head, and, with a deep breath, took off running.

She was glad she'd chosen her flat boots today instead of the heels she usually wore to the office, but she was also hating herself for picking up the cigarettes again, and for the second time that week, she vowed to get to the gym more often. She blended in with all the other people running down the street away from gunfire and finally heard police sirens. She didn't hear gunshots anymore, but she didn't stop, and she didn't look back.

By the time she reached the front of the police station on 20th, she felt like her lungs were going to explode.

There was a flurry of activity around her, cops running everywhere. People screaming. Panic was quick in the city when anything out of the ordinary happened these days. Everyone's first thought was terrorism. She lowered herself onto the steps in front of the building by the railing and tried to catch her breath. In all the activity, it was a few minutes before anyone noticed her.

The cop in front of her was shaking a hand in her face and shaking her shoulder for who knew how long before she came back to herself enough to answer him.

"Ma'am, ma'am, are you hurt? Were you shot?" His grip on her upper arms where he held her hurt, and she quickly pushed them off.

"I'm okay," she said almost to herself, barely believing it. Then, with more confidence, she looked him in the eye. "I'm okay. I wasn't shot. But the gunman rammed my car. And then he started shooting, and I just ran…."

"You did good. You're safe now. Let's get you inside."

"You have to call Detective Justus. He's at the 10th precinct. This could be connected to a case. I think someone just tried to kill me."

She could tell for a moment that the officer was having a hard time believing her. She could imagine what she must look like, blood dripping down her face and shaking.

"Fine, we'll call him. But first, we're going to take you inside and have someone check you out. You're bleeding. All right?"

"Sure," she said. "Okay."

She made it. She was safe.

CHAPTER THIRTY-THREE

YOU GRABBED YOUR PURSE?

WILL arrived at the police station agitated and not bothering to try to hide it. When he'd received the call from the officer who'd taken care of Cameron, he immediately thought the worst. He'd heard the reports on the police scanner—everyone had—and seen the initial reports on the news. Shots fired in the city, but he had no idea she could've been involved.

He stopped at the crime scene on his way to meet her, comfortable delaying his arrival once he was assured she wasn't seriously hurt. It was a mess. Her car was destroyed, the whole side caved in. The truck that hit her wasn't much better, the whole front almost crushed up to the interior. It appeared to have pushed her halfway down the block before a taxi had struck it.

Will introduced himself and had gotten a brief from one of the detectives on the scene. The truck was stolen. The

CSI team was working on the trace from the interior, but they hadn't caught the perpetrator; he was still on the run. The local news media was already reporting on the incident. Thankfully, no one had been killed. But there had meant to be. The shooter, whoever he was, had meant to kill Cameron.

When he finally spotted her, she was sitting in a chair. A medic with a penlight was shining it in her eyes, he assumed checking her for signs of a concussion. He could see dried blood traces on her face but nothing on her clothes. She was dressed in typical New York fashion in all black, which was effective in hiding bloodstains. He bet she hadn't planned on that when she picked out her outfit.

An officer was standing beside her when he approached, and he reached out his hand in greeting.

"Officer DeFilippo?" he asked.

"Yes, you must be Detective Justus."

"I am." He shifted his gaze to Cameron. "You okay?"

"I'm fine." She nodded, her answer a little shaky. "Just some scratches, a few stitches, and a lot of bruises."

"Sir," Officer DeFilippo said. "Our captain would like to speak to you for a minute if you don't mind."

"No problem. Will you be all right for a few minutes?" She nodded back. "Wait for me right here, please," he instructed before following the officer down the hall.

The captain's office looked remarkably similar to his captain's. Although he guessed it wasn't too surprising. All the police stations in the city had the same feel. Outdated equipment and files piled everywhere. Décor that felt like it was from the '70s. It seemed like cosmetic upgrades were never in the budget.

The meeting with the 13th precinct's captain didn't take long. Since there was so little evidence in both their cases, it wasn't time-consuming to share. The longest amount of time spent together was after the captain had sent a picture of the suspect in Cameron's shooting to the detectives in the New Jersey hit-and-run case of Cameron's friend. Waiting for the detective to call back was like torture. But he did, and they had their first break. Despite the criminal's efforts to cover his face, they had him on camera a few blocks away from the scene, ripping his mask off before heading down into the subway, and they were able to get a picture. The Bergen County police were able to match it to the suspect in Casey Keane's murder.

Will left the office feeling like they were finally making real progress and with a copy of the photo in his hand. He just wasn't happy about what had happened to Cameron to get them there. If she'd been killed, well, he didn't even want to think about it. He'd had a good time talking with her the night before. No, it was more than good. Sharing a drink with her was easy but exciting as well. She was interesting and thoughtful in a way it seemed most people weren't. He couldn't imagine her dead. Especially not because of a case he couldn't solve.

Cameron was still sitting where he'd left her, smiling and drinking a soda with a young officer.

"Time to go," he said abruptly, not even glancing at the other man.

"All right, let me just grab my stuff." She reached down

to straighten the messenger bag she always carried for work.

"Your stuff?"

"Yeah, my bag," she replied, looking puzzled at his tone, holding the strap up for him to see.

He blinked, unable to process what she had said for a moment. "Let me get this straight. A man is shooting at you, you're literally running for your life, and you stopped to grab your purse?"

"Hey, man," the officer put in. "Go easy on her. She's had a rough morning."

Will's entire body stiffened, and he moved nothing but his head. He looked like a really tall owl as he turned to face the man. "Go away."

The officer must have read something on his face because without another word, he turned and walked away.

***

"Well, that was rude," Cameron noted.

"Rude? Fuck rude! You were almost killed. I don't have time to deal with Romeo's feelings. We've got to get moving."

"Where are we going?" she asked apprehensively. She'd never seen him this worked up, and it was unnerving.

"To your place so you can shower and change clothes. Get that blood off you. Then back to the office. We've got new leads and those interviews today. Are you still up for it?"

"I don't know," she replied hesitantly but honestly. "I mean, watching interviews was one thing, but my apartment was broken into, and I was shot at today. I think I've reached my limit, and I know I'm way out of my depth here."

Things were moving too fast. She needed to slow down, get back to something close to normal. She would feel more guilt at not seeing it through, not getting justice for Casey, but she'd already lost her job. She didn't want to lose her life.

"I understand. You might still be a little in shock, and whether you listen in on the interviews or not, the safest place for you right now is with me. At the station."

"Okay. I guess the best way to end this is to see it through," she said with as much conviction as she could muster, but she felt as if there was a massive rock in her stomach, and until the killer was caught, she didn't think it was going anywhere.

CHAPTER THIRTY-FOUR

YOU CAN'T GO HOME AGAIN. WELL, YOU CAN,
BUT THE MAGIC CLEANING ELVES STILL
HAVEN'T VISITED.

THEY left the station and walked the two blocks to her apartment. This walk felt so much different than their stroll through Manhattan the night before. It felt like a lifetime ago to Cameron. It was amazing how much difference a few hours could make. The air was just as crisp, but the feeling on the city streets was completely different. There was no feeling of promise in the air as there had been. Just a pronounced sense of silence making the streets feel desolate and somehow foreboding. And even though the danger had passed, Cameron could still sense it all around.

Even entering her apartment didn't dispel any of her anxiety. It was still a mess from the break-in, and it was just another reminder of the strange situation she found herself in. It had been less than a week since she made the discovery that put her there, and she couldn't believe how quickly her life had changed.

She dropped her bag at the entrance as she always did while Will moved past her and settled himself on her couch, making himself at home. She started to make her way to her bathroom and stopped.

"What is it?" he asked softly.

"Nothing. I just realized showering will be tricky. I can't get my hair wet." She gestured to her forehead. "Stitches. Can't get it wet for twenty-four hours."

"Let me see." As he motioned her toward him, she moved without a thought.

It should've been strange, being so close to a man she barely knew. But it wasn't. It felt natural, easy, like she'd known him for years. She'd dated men for months and never felt this comfortable with them. It must have been the extreme situation. Shared experiences always caused a feeling of closeness. It would go away. She wouldn't take it too seriously.

She sat on the coffee table in front of her bright red couch that Will had scooted to the front of. He lifted his hand to touch her forehead where the cut was, and she winced.

"They did a pretty good job considering," he said, his breath soft and surprisingly fresh against her face. "Why didn't you let them take you to the hospital?"

It took her a few seconds to respond, so disoriented from his closeness.

"It's not that bad. I already had a scar there from when

I was a kid, so I wasn't worried about that. It was just two stitches. The paramedic did it at the station."

"Ah, a tough girl."

His hand was still touching her face, although there seemed no reason for it to be. And it made her nervous. He was undeniably attractive, and Cameron had noticed. Being this close to him, it was hard not to stare. His focus still seemed to be on her scar, but she wondered what he was thinking. Was he attracted? Or was he just concerned, considering she'd been hurt? It was impossible to tell.

"Not so much. I just had a lot of stitches when I was young. The scar that's there was from running into a brick wall."

His lips tilted up into an amused smile, and he was still touching her face.

"You ran into a wall?"

"I was chasing my dog. It's a long story," she babbled, shifting her weight between her feet. His face was so close to hers. If he just turned a little bit….

Was he going to kiss her? Did she want him to?

But at that, he seemed to notice their closeness and withdrew swiftly, sliding to the back of the couch and putting as much space between them as he could.

"Well, it looks good. Be careful cleaning up. You don't want to get it infected."

It was said harshly in comparison to the soft, almost breathy way he'd been speaking to her. She felt the difference in her chest.

Well, that answered that question. He did not feel the

attraction. That was okay; maybe he had someone in his life. She hadn't even thought to ask. Hopefully they'd soon find the murderer, and then they'd go their separate ways.

It was for the best, she thought as she got up silently and made her way to the bathroom. She didn't need the distraction, and his career was just as demanding as hers with as crazy hours, it seemed. She'd had a brief moment of fantasy, and with the way he looked, what woman wouldn't? She imagined he'd understand her devotion to her career because he was equally invested. And a man like him certainly wouldn't be intimidated by the fact that she worked primarily with men.

She glanced back before walking through the doorway into the bathroom and found him studiously looking at his phone.

Yep, not interested.

CHAPTER THIRTY-FIVE

ONE DOWN

STEPPING out of the elevator onto the third floor of the police station, Cameron was struck by the activity. There weren't this many people here on any of her other visits. She got the feeling something was happening. Her intuition was confirmed when Captain Lovett poked his head out of the conference room he'd been in to shout at them.

"Justus, where have you been? Get in here."

"What's going on?" she asked as they hustled past the cubicles.

"No idea," Will answered. "But I bet we're about to find out."

Detective Jones's head whipped up as soon as they stepped into the room. Captain Lovett and ADA Goodrich were gathered around the conference table, intently poring over some papers. Alan's eye settled on her bruised and scarred face, a sympathetic look crossing his features before he responded.

"We've got him," he stated excitedly. "Well, I doubt it's the person behind all of this, but the man who shot at you, Ms. Caldwell, and killed your friend, possibly Mr. Rodriguez, but that's doubtful. Looks like he's just the cleanup crew."

Cameron fell into a chair, dropping her head in her hands. Relief filled her body with the exhalation of breath. She was safe. Or maybe not, but surely soon. They'd find out who hired him quickly, and then she would be. And Casey's killer would be brought to justice. She'd been ignoring her feelings about his death for the last few days, afraid she'd fall apart, but the end was almost there.

She came back to herself and realized she'd been missing the conversation.

"We got him from the New Jersey boys on the hit-and-run. They're bringing him in as we speak. Hopefully he'll make a deal to tell us who hired him. If not, I imagine we'll find out quickly. According to the detectives over there, he's not exactly a brain trust. He's a repeat offender. They recognized him as soon as they got his picture," the captain said.

"Are they bringing him down here?" Will asked.

"No," answered Kim. "Jersey's got him on murder charges. We've only got attempted, so they'll file charges there. They're being extremely cooperative, mostly because that picture you sent them was the confirmation they needed to get a warrant for their suspect. We can interrogate him there if we like. But they know what we're looking for and will try to get it for us."

Will looked like he was going to argue, but the captain cut him off first.

"I know you want this guy, but this is for the best."

"I want to go to Jersey and talk to this guy," Will responded with a growl.

"No," Cameron answered, startling them all. She imagined they'd almost forgotten she was there. "He didn't kill Rodriguez, so it still has to be one of them," she said, gesturing to the whiteboard with the suspects listed on it. "They don't get to get away with it and let this guy take the blame. Wait, what's his name? I don't want to keep calling him 'that guy.'"

"His name's Toby Tucker. He's had a series of entry-level jobs. No real education, barely made it through high school." Alan stuck his picture up on the board, and she nodded. So that was who killed Casey. It was so unreal to think that such a brilliant man in the prime of his life had been wiped out by this loser.

"You have to stay here and do the interviews. Chances are it's either Wells or Reece who hired him, right? I mean, you don't think it was Trey, do you?" Cameron asked.

"No," Will answered thoughtfully, leaning up against the wall. "He never felt right for it. I shared your theories with the team," he added.

She nodded in acknowledgment.

"What about you?" Kim asked, nodding at Alan.

"I didn't either. Something about it just didn't sit right. With all the research you dug up on him, I couldn't find anything that would suggest he had that kind of violence in him. His few brushes with the law were all alcohol-related when he was young, stupid stuff, nothing of consequence."

"I agree," said the captain. "She's right. It's probably one of them. And if the New Jersey cops can't get the killer's identity out of their suspect, we need you here to interrogate them. The hit man may not be smart, but these SE people are."

"They're not as smart as they think they are," said Will, a stiffness in his jaw settling in with determination. "I say we make them wait. Let's see what the Jersey cops can get. It'll be a whole different ball game if they can get us a name. In the meantime, let's look through the information they sent. Maybe we can find a connection to one of our suspects."

CHAPTER THIRTY-SIX

IT COULDN'T BE THAT SIMPLE, COULD IT?

IT was a few minutes past three by the time Will and Kim entered the interrogation room containing Tessa Wells and her attorney. He could see her irritation, and this time she was making no attempt to hide it. Gone was the delicate waif he'd seen at the SE offices. In front of him sat a tough, defiant woman. And she clearly didn't feel the need for the disguise anymore.

They sat slowly, not feeling the need to rush, laying out folders and files in front of them on the table. Her irritation continued to grow at their lack of urgency, and Will thought if he played it just right, he could probably get her to snap. She had the look of a woman used to getting her way, and that wasn't the way it worked in this room.

"Ms. Wells, thank you for coming down. We're sorry for the delay," Will led the questioning. "You remember ADA Goodrich, don't you?"

She nodded in response sharply, but before she could speak, her lawyer cut in.

"Detective, this is completely unprofessional. You asked my client to come down here, and then you keep her waiting for over an hour, treating her as if she's a criminal. I hope you'll handle this interview with more finesse than you've shown so far."

"Oh, I'm sure we will," he answered lightly, ruffling the stiff lawyer's feathers a bit by not taking his warning as seriously as he intended. "But before we get started, I'd like to confirm Ms. Wells was read her rights prior to this interview?"

"Again, completely unnecessary, but my client has been advised of her rights. May I ask why the assistant district attorney is participating in this interview? It seems a bit irregular."

"Of course," answered Kim. "Due to the high-profile nature of this case, the department wants to make sure all their ducks are in a row and no mistakes are made that might hamper prosecution once an arrest is made. I'm sure your client would agree with that. I mean, doesn't she want her friend's murder prosecuted to the fullest extent of the law?"

"Of course I do!" exclaimed Tessa. "This whole thing with Matt has just been awful. I'm just ready for this to be over."

"I understand, Tessa," Will said sympathetically. "If you can just answer some questions for us and clear some things up, we'll be able to make our arrest."

"You know who did it?" she asked, eyes wide, not breathing.

"We have a strong suspect," he confirmed, noting her rising anxiety and her swift glance at her attorney. He was sure her lawyer didn't miss it either if the shift in his posture was anything to go by.

"Ms. Wells," Will began, pulling out an evidence bag containing the chip Cameron had found. "Have you ever seen this before?"

"No," she answered quickly. "Well, I don't think so. Not that one specifically. It's a computer chip. Looks just like the millions of chips I've seen."

"I see," he said, moving on. Pulling a stack of pictures out of the file, he laid them in front of her on the desk. "And on the Friday night in question, you took a helicopter out to the Hamptons with Mr. Howell and Mr. Reece in the afternoon and didn't return to the city until the following Sunday, is that correct?"

"Yes, I've told you this. What are these pictures of?"

"These are pictures people took at the SE party at Trey's house that night. It was nice of him to hire a professional photographer to capture such a momentous occasion for SE. We got their pictures too. We've examined all of them. I'm not much for technology myself, certainly not like you and your friends, but even I know all pictures taken nowadays have a date and time stamp embedded in them. The metadata, I guess they call it."

She was beginning to sweat a bit, he could tell. She didn't expect this, he was sure.

"And? I was there. I'm sure I'm in some of those photos."

"You are," he agreed, nodding. "But no matter how hard

we searched, we couldn't find any pictures of you between 8:00 p.m. and 10:30 p.m."

"So?" she replied, waving her lawyer off when he attempted to answer for her. "It was a big group, and it's a big house. I'm sure there are lots of people who weren't in all the pictures."

"Okay. Then have you ever used a charter helicopter company that provides a shuttle service from Manhattan to the Hamptons called Hampton Sky Taxi?

"No," she whispered, her face going white.

He pulled another set of papers from his file. "I apologize again for the delay in our interview today, but we were interviewing a pilot from one of the helicopters from that service. He was flying Friday night, and he remembers you. He states that he took you back to the city on the 8:30 p.m. flight and then returned you to the Hamptons on the 10:00 p.m. flight. He remembers you because you paid in cash."

"Hearsay," interjected her lawyer. "How reliable is this witness?"

"Well," Will said, "he's a medal of honor recipient who will swear under oath that she was on those flights."

"That still doesn't put her at the crime scene," the lawyer said, though most of his bravado was gone at this point.

"You're right, it doesn't, but we have no doubt we can get a conviction when we present the motive," he said, nodding at Kim, who nodded back.

"What motive?" Tessa asked, a little of her bravado creeping back into her voice. "Matt was my friend. I had no reason to kill him. I loved him."

"I think you did love him," he replied. "I think you love all of them. They were your family, right? You needed them. Your father committed suicide when you were five, correct? And then your mother left you, traveled all the time. She left you with nannies and sent you to boarding school. I bet being with Trey, Brandon, Matt, and Mark was the closest thing to a family you ever had."

"Yes, exactly," she responded, a hint of desperation seeping into her voice. "I would never hurt my family."

"You would if someone was threatening to take it all away, wouldn't you, Tessa?"

"What are you talking about? Matt would never hurt me."

Will picked up the evidence bag on the table again, watching Tessa's eyes track the chip in the bag as it swung in his hand.

"He found your chip, Tessa. He was going to tell Trey. And when he did, it would all be over. You'd lose your job, your friends, your family, and it would ruin Synergistic," he stressed. "You couldn't let him do that, could you?"

"That's enough," her lawyer cut in. "Either charge my client or we're leaving."

"All right. Tessa Wells, you're under arrest for the murder of Matteo Rodriguez. You have the right to remain silent."

He finished reading her Miranda rights while she stared at him seething. It wasn't the response he'd anticipated. Usually, when suspects knew they'd been caught, they cried or showed remorse. Tessa Wells just looked pissed.

"Do you understand these rights?"

"You've got nothing," she hissed at him. "My lawyers will make you look like a fool. You can't prove I did anything."

He sighed and gave her a pitying look. "The police in New Jersey have arrested your friend Toby Tucker. He gave you up. He was your nanny's nephew. You knew him as a kid. So, when you discovered your chips had been found, you sent him on the cleanup mission. He's being charged with the murder of Casey Keane in New Jersey and attempted murder in New York. He wasn't successful on the second mission. But he did still have all the money you paid him with and the envelope it came in. They're running it for prints now."

"It's circumstantial," the lawyer said. "They were childhood friends. That money could've been for anything."

He was posturing. Will could tell the lawyer knew they were in trouble. But Tessa's face never changed. Her arrogance shone through clear now, and it was obvious to him that she thought she'd covered all her bases and she'd get away with it.

"And then there's this," he said, lifting the chip again. "It took a while, but our techs finally traced where the transmissions from the chip were being sent, and they found your cloud account. It still contained all the data from all your chips. The ones you planted on Matt and Mark, but also the ones you planted on Trey and Brandon. Turns out you were spying on all your boyfriends. Not the trusting sort, are you, Tessa? Every bit of information you gathered was there."

"It's meaningless," she said. "Someone's setting me up. I didn't do anything, and you can't prove I did."

Will smiled, savoring the moment. Usually, he wasn't this vindictive, or at least he didn't like to think so, but he was going to enjoy putting Tessa Wells away. She'd tried to kill Cameron, and that didn't sit well with him. Plus, her continued defiance grated on him. She truly believed she was above all of this and that she'd be walking out of here free and clear. Well, it was time to dissuade her of that notion for good.

"That could be true except for one thing, Tessa. When Matt discovered your chips, he didn't get rid of his HomeTech Hub. He took it to his office. Cameras in the SE offices recorded you murdering him, and the HTH uploaded the data and transmitted it at midnight as you programmed it to do. You deleted the local NVR information from the camera at SE, but the info had already been shared with your chip in the HomeTech Hub. The file was still there when our techs got in. I don't know if you overlooked it, or if you're sick enough to have wanted to watch it yourself. You caught yourself, Tessa. Game over."

The look on her face was priceless.

Kim wasted no time. She turned to the attorney, completely overlooking Tessa. She was of no use to her now. Her social status gone; there was no reason for Kim to be interested in her. "We'll be charging her with murder one. She'll get life, no possibility of parole."

With that, Will and Kim both got up to leave.

That was when Tessa finally lost it. She began screaming at them as her attorney tried to hold her back. It was a lot of "You can't do this to me" and "Don't you know who I am?" Things Will had heard before. They didn't stop or acknowledge her; he just walked out of the room and nodded at the officer waiting there. He waited for them to exit, then made his way in to arrest her. He'd get her processed, and she'd be in a cell tonight. It was doubtful she'd get bail or ever breathe free again. It was a good day's work. He could put the case to rest and leave Kim to handle it from here on. He was confident she'd get a conviction. The evidence was solid. It wasn't every day they had a video of the murder. It'd be a big case for Kim, and high-profile cases were what she lived for.

They got back to the conference room, and Cameron and Alan were waiting for them.

"I'm going to head on to my office," Kim said, hovering in the doorway, not quite entering the room. "I want to get everything set for the arraignment. That bitch isn't getting bail if I can help it. It's been good seeing you, Will, Alan. Cameron, my office will be in touch. You'll have to testify."

And with that, she was gone.

Looking at his watch, Will noted there was time for Kim to give a statement for the afternoon news. Typical. He imagined they'd see a lot of her in the media over the next few months. She'd love that.

"Well, that should be pleasant," Cameron said from her spot at the table. "So, is it over?"

"It's over." Will nodded. "You're safe now."

Relief filled Cameron's features, and she blew out a deep breath. "Thank you."

"I'm going to go grab the rest of those evidence logs, Will. I'll be back in a bit. Cameron, good to meet you, and thank you for the help." Alan reached out to shake her hand. "You're one tough lady."

He walked out the door, leaving them alone.

Uncomfortable in the silence, Cameron moved to start gathering up her things.

"I was thinking," Will said, stopping her. "Tomorrow's Friday, and my caseload has suddenly lightened up. You aren't working. Maybe you'd like to grab lunch?"

"That'd be great," she said, smiling back at him.

* * *

She was feeling good as she boarded the elevator at the station. Casey's murderer was caught; she was as safe as she could be. She could begin to put this whole thing behind her, and Will wanted to see her again. That was an unexpected bonus. She'd go to the funeral on Saturday, mourn with their friends, and Monday she'd go see Steve about getting her job back. Things weren't perfect. It would take her a while to work through everything that had happened. But now she could see the light at the end of the tunnel. She'd never thought much about justice before, but there was a sense of relief that came with knowing the murderer was caught. She wished all victims could feel this way.

She boarded the elevator without paying much attention until someone spoke to her.

"You're Cameron, aren't you?" she heard from the back of the elevator. "Cameron Caldwell?"

"Yeah," she answered, turning. And found herself face-to-face with Trey Howell.

He must have seen the panic on her face because he was quick to reassure her.

"Don't be upset. I'm sorry. I'm just…," he said, exhaling and leaning back against the rear of the elevator. "I'm just… well, they told me what happened, what she did. I guess I'm just trying to get my head around it. I don't understand. This will ruin us. She destroyed everything. And for what? I just don't get it."

Cameron stopped and considered him for a minute. He seemed genuinely distraught. Gone was the polished professional she'd watched in the interrogation room.

"I don't know that you'll ever find a satisfactory answer," she said cautiously. "You probably knew her best, but from everything they found, it seemed she was a very sad woman. And very lonely. She just wanted a family and went about it the wrong way."

He was nodding along. "Her father messed her up. She'd talk about him sometimes, you know. She spent all her holidays with my family growing up, and we weren't the most stable. Looking back, it seems to make some sense, I guess. But how could she do this to me? To the company? To everything we built? We worked so hard, and now it's over. No one will want a HomeTech Hub after this gets out. Synergistic is ruined."

The doors opened out onto the main floor, and Cameron

was relieved. She didn't know what else to say to him, and it was an uncomfortable conversation to be having with a man she'd never met before.

"Thanks for listening. I'm sorry to just let it out on you like that," he said, composing himself, then giving a short laugh. "Unreal. She recorded herself killing him, and she saved it? Unbelievable."

And then he walked away. Trey Howell would have a lot to deal with come morning. But whatever became of Synergistic Engineering was no longer her problem.

He was right about one thing. If she stopped to consider it, Tessa Wells recording herself committing murder was unbelievable.

CHAPTER THIRTY-SEVEN

LOOSE ENDS SINK SHIPS

CAMERON was on edge before meeting Will for lunch at her favorite restaurant in the Flatiron district. She'd spent the night before getting her apartment back in order. Which mostly consisted of her throwing things out. She'd lost count of how many trash bags she'd taken to the garbage room. It was going to be hard replacing everything she'd lost without the income from her job. Hopefully her homeowner's insurance would cover some of the damage, but she wasn't sure if her policy covered crazed murderers.

She was hoping her meeting on Monday with Steve would go well and she could get her life back on track. They could easily spin SmartTech's involvement in the HTH scandal in a positive manner. SmartTech, so secure they identified and shut down a billion-dollar product market just to keep their customers safe from hacking. The marketing spin practically wrote itself, which was a bonus because

SmartTech's marketing team wasn't known as the best in the industry.

It also helped that Mark Minsky wasn't making a fuss. Wasn't even upset. He was thanking Barry and SmartTech by extension for their diligence in finding his security breach. Barry was thrilled. He had a client for life and referrals galore. His business would skyrocket. Everyone was coming out of this well. Except for her. And Casey.

She shook off those thoughts as she dug her hands deeper into her coat pockets. The weather had taken a colder turn heading into the weekend, and she'd been unable to find her gloves in all the mess. It was earlier in the season than she usually used them as it was, but with the mess in her apartment, finding anything was a lost cause.

She saw Will waiting in front of the restaurant as she turned the corner and took a minute to take him in. He was standing off to the side of the door, scanning the crowd as people passed. She was sure it was a side effect of his profession or a holdover from his military years. Always a cop searching for anomalies in the herd.

She greeted him with a smile, and he opened the door for her, ushering her into the restaurant with a hand on her back. He even pulled out her chair for her when the hostess sat them, waving her away from the task, choosing to do it himself. She liked it. The gentlemanly gestures were so foreign to her. She hadn't had a man treat her with that sort of deference in longer than she could remember.

They made pleasantries for a bit, and she waited until they ordered to broach the subject that had been on her mind all night.

"I met Trey Howell yesterday in the elevator leaving your office," she said casually.

"Oh really?" he asked curiously. "How did that go?"

"It was odd. He seemed upset, but he said some things that got me thinking."

"Like what?" He raised an eyebrow at her.

"Well, for one thing, how did he know who I was? I never actually met anyone from Synergistic. I can't imagine anyone on your team would've told him of my involvement, so how did he know?"

Will thought for a minute and sipped his tea. "Mark Minsky," he answered confidently. "He knew. We told him as much during our first interview, and he could've gotten more information from your customer at Digital Lifestyles. It wouldn't have been hard for someone like Trey to put the pieces together."

She considered it for a moment and then conceded his point. It made sense. A logical solution.

"Okay, then tell me this. The last thing he said to me was that it was unbelievable that Tessa got rid of all the electronic evidence of her crime but left the recording from the HomeTech Hub. It is kind of hard to get my head around. She was so careful to erase all the video, his hard drive, and all their servers. Why leave that piece of evidence?"

"Maybe she didn't know it was recorded?"

"She had to if she was the one reviewing the data from the chips. She went after Matt because he'd discovered the chips. To know that, she'd have to have been tracking his hub and known that he'd taken it from his apartment back to his office. It's not rational to think she wouldn't have seen it and gotten rid of the data when it uploaded to her cloud."

"Maybe she didn't look at Matt's uploads since she murdered him and had no idea he'd even brought the hub to the office? It follows, then, that she wouldn't have even know it passed along the recording. She didn't have any reason to look at his data anymore. And why would she think an HTH in his office would be significant if she did see it? They have to have them all over the place. They all look identical, and she didn't have all night to mess around at the scene. She had to get back to the party in the Hamptons before anyone missed her."

"True, but that's the other thing. How realistic is it that neither Trey nor Brandon noticed her gone from the party for so long? In everything we found about them, it showed they were thick as thieves. I can't see how she was gone for three hours and they didn't notice."

"What are you saying? You think they were in it together?"

"They had to be. At least two of them," she stated confidently. "She may have been able to design and program the chip, but to put it all together like that, it would've taken more than her basic skills."

"She confessed, Cameron. She didn't implicate anyone else. It's over."

She stared at him for a minute, not appreciating his dismissive tone. "And then there's this." She reached into her bag and pulled out a copy of an article.

"What is this?" he asked, taking it from her.

"It's an article I found. It was written for the school newspaper at MIT when Trey Howell was a student. It's a review of a roundtable they had about the effects of technology and privacy laws. It focused on the government's inability to keep up with necessary legislation because technology evolves too quickly to be properly regulated."

"So?" he said, skimming the article.

"Trey Howell was a panelist. They quoted him. I highlighted it for you."

He looked down at the paper and began to read the section she'd indicated. "Government will always be a step behind technology. With the general public's fascination increasing at an astronomical rate, the law will continue to fall farther and farther behind. With the advent of more home technology than ever before, it's most likely that we'll see a future where individual privacy is nothing more than an illusion. And this will happen sooner than you would think."

He finished reading and looked at her.

"He was describing using the HomeTech Hub as spyware, and he did it fifteen years ago," she said excitedly. "He did this."

"Cameron, this is an old article. Lots of MIT students probably said the same thing. It doesn't mean anything." He said it patiently, but she found it condescending.

"He did this. Tessa is in love with him. She'd cover for him. Maybe she was sleeping with the others to try to make him jealous, looking for data from the hubs to put cracks in their relationships. Create division, bring Trey closer to her. But whatever the reason she was doing it, he was talking about using home technology as spyware fifteen years ago. He recruited Matt Rodriguez for this. He was planning this. You said it yourself, he's the leader. The others just followed him. But Matt didn't know about the plan, and they had to get him out of the way. Tessa was just the means to the end."

"There's no proof, Cameron. We have the video. She confessed. It's over. You need to let this go. You sound like a conspiracy theorist raving about little green men. Like those guys on *The X-Files*."

She snorted, rolling her eyes. "The Lone Gunmen," she stated wistfully.

"No, there were three of them."

She shook her head at him, disappointed by his unwillingness to believe her and saddened by the reminder of her banter with Casey. "Then answer me this. Why delete all of Matt's files, the hard drives, all of it? Did Tessa ever say what he found? He had something, some proof. Find that and you can nail Trey Howell. Tessa's insecurity and her family issues are just a red herring. There's something else going on here."

"A red herring? Now you've moved away from *Law and Order* and entered Agatha Christie territory." He must have noticed the anger rising in her expression, as he hurriedly moved on. "It doesn't matter anyway. There's nothing left to find."

"Look, I know technology isn't your thing, but it's mine. This chip, this whole concept. Implanting spyware in a device that can access every bit of data you touch. Most people aren't even aware they're providing it. This has tremendously far-reaching implications. Huge financial implications. There is no way that this was all about one woman's jealousy. I'm back to my original theory. This was a beta test. Once they had accurate data over a period of time from several devices, they could sell this. Calculate accurately how much storage they'd need to make it efficient, put a budget in place for staff, etc. This was the beginning of a business plan. Trey Howell had this idea before he recruited Matt Rodriguez to Synergistic. They just used his HTH as a delivery system. It was the perfect Trojan horse. He created this with Tessa, but he was the one receiving the data. That's why she didn't know the murder had been recorded. He set her up to take the fall. And she's so brainwashed by love or whatever, she's doing it. I don't know what the master plan here is, but I bet Matt found out. If we can find out what he knew, you'll have them. You have to find his cloud account."

"Yes, they got that too."

"All of them?" she asked.

"What do you mean, all of them? He only had one."

"Was it a personal or business account?"

"It was a Synergistic account, why?"

"Then he had at least one other account," she stated confidently.

"We checked. He didn't have any other cloud accounts registered to him on any service we could find."

"He had another one. Trust me, Will, he had a personal account."

He sighed, and it irked her. It felt patronizing. He took a deep breath, and she knew whatever he had to say next wasn't because he believed her, it was because he was placating her.

"How can you be so sure?"

She was right. That even, still tone he used was filled with pity, and it was condescending. She didn't need to know him long to recognize that.

"Because," she snapped back, suddenly furious, "everybody has a personal cloud account. It's where you keep all your documents, your taxes, leases, insurance stuff. Stuff you don't want your boss to see, porn. No one, especially someone as technically astute as Matt Rodriguez, wouldn't. You do it in case you change jobs and lose access to your work account. Salespeople always save a client list in case they get fired and don't want to lose all their contacts. Maybe your guys couldn't find it, but it's out there, and the proof you need is on it. Plus, I'm positive he had an account in college. He went to MIT, for God's sake. All students have one. It's probably still active."

He seemed a little shocked at her vehemence, and maybe she was being a little too aggressive. But the truth was she knew there was more to this story than cyberstalking. And the more Will dismissed her, the more frustrated she got.

"Don't you want to know what Matt found? What got him killed?" she asked softly. "Even if it wasn't Trey, and Tessa acted alone, don't you want to know why?"

He stared at her for a minute, not speaking, assessing. "We know why, Cameron. She was obsessed. She's not sane. She was so paranoid the men in her life were going to leave her, she had to track their every movement just to feel secure in her position with them. And Matt found out and tried to take it all away. That's why she killed him. It's just that simple. Look, I know you're at loose ends. You lost your job, you lost a friend, and being involved this week has helped. Been cathartic for you. But it's over now. You need to let it go."

She was saved from answering too quickly by the waiter bringing their plates. By the time he walked away, she'd put away her anger and was mostly feeling disappointed.

"You know, I thought you were the kind of cop who would see this through." She reached into her bag, grabbed two twenties, and threw them on the table. "There's evidence out there, Will, and regardless of what it'll prove, it's a loose end. People have died. I almost died. Don't you think we deserve the truth?"

And with that, she walked out. She'd be lying if she said she wasn't disappointed that he didn't even try to stop her.

CHAPTER THIRTY-EIGHT

"I'M SORRY" AND "MY BAD" MEAN THE SAME
THING. UNLESS YOU'RE AT A FUNERAL.

FUNERALS   were never fun. She'd gotten a rental car
from her insurance company the day before and had planned
to keep it for at least a few weeks until she could buy a
new Jeep. She'd covered up the stitches on her forehead to
the best of her ability, but she knew they still looked awful.
The service was crowded with people from SmartTech, and
Cameron could feel some of the looks she got were less
than friendly, but Bill and Phil stood by her side, and the
coworkers who did speak to her were kind. She'd gotten
so many strange looks during the service at the church, she
couldn't tell if they were staring at the bandage or if it was
her residual guilt making her feel judged. She wouldn't have
made it through without her team. They met her outside the
church and didn't leave her alone for a minute. It hurt seeing
people who were her friends and colleagues a few days ago

standing in groups together whispering about her. She could only imagine the gossip and what rumors were spreading.

The service seemed to last forever. It was an insanely long Catholic production, and the longer she sat on the hard wooden pew, the more she felt like the walls of the cathedral were closing in on her. Anxiety crept in when she saw Steve, and the hard stare he gave her ate at her until she thought she couldn't breathe. It was a relief when it was over; she had to will herself to keep a steady pace next to Bill and Phil and not sprint out the door. It was so painful that she debated not going on to the cemetery, but she knew she couldn't live with herself if she did. She wasn't a coward; she hadn't stopped searching for Casey's killer even after she'd been attacked, and she wouldn't let fear push her away from saying her final goodbye either. He was her friend; he deserved that respect.

Standing in the cold, wet New Jersey morning with Bill and Phil, waiting for Casey's casket to be lowered into the ground, made her feel so lost. The chill and the drizzle in the air made a sober occasion feel even more desolate. His wife hadn't stopped crying since she'd arrived, newborn in tow. Several people she assumed were family had tried to step in and take the baby away, but she held tight, not wanting to let even that small piece of Casey she had left go. It was heartrending.

Cameron stayed away from Casey's family. She didn't know what she would've said, what they may have known about her involvement in his death. Maybe that was cowardly, but she just couldn't face it. She was disappointed in herself enough for the day and didn't want to add to it. She'd failed to convince Will that the case was still unfinished, and upon arriving at the church and seeing Casey's widow, she couldn't remember if his kid was a boy or a girl. What kind of friend did that make her? She was sure the team had sent a gift for the baby shower. She knew she'd gotten something off the registry and sent it from the three of them, but for the life of her, she couldn't even remember the baby's sex, much less its name. She was feeling shitty all around.

"C'mon, kid," Bill said after the service, putting his arm around her. "Let's get out of here and grab a drink."

"It's only noon," she replied.

"So we'll get Bloody Marys. Come on, I bet you didn't even have breakfast. Phil, man, you in?"

"Yeah, just let me go tell Misty where I'm going."

This prompted an eye roll from Bill and a smile from Cameron.

"What's with the eye roll? You don't like Misty?" she asked.

"I like Misty fine. I just can't believe he jumped right back into a relationship so soon after his divorce."

"He's happy, and that's the important thing. Besides, not everybody wants to be out with a different girl every night like you. Some people like being in relationships."

"Whatever," Bill answered, steering her toward the parking lot. "Let's go get that drink."

CHAPTER THIRTY-NINE

TEAMWORK MAKES THE DREAM WORK

THEY went to an Irish pub located near the office. It was a comfortable spot where the work crew gathered after work at times for drinks to celebrate the end of a quarter if they did particularly well. And they made a killer brunch as well as fancy Bloody Marys with all the fixings, which all three of them ordered immediately upon sitting in their usual booth.

It reminded Cameron of her dinner earlier that week with Will, and that made her sad. Just days ago they were working together to solve the crime, and now she was on her own. Her disappointment in him was almost a tangible thing. She'd thought better of him. It wasn't rational, but his refusal to believe that they hadn't yet gotten the whole story had let her down. Such an unrealistic expectation of someone she'd just met.

They shrugged off all the layers they had put on to brave

the cold that morning by the gravesite and stuffed them in her side of the booth as the boys packed in on the other side together.

"All right, kid, something is on your mind. Is it the job thing? I'm sure once you talk to Steve on Monday, that'll all get resolved," Phil said.

She nodded, appreciative of his support although she didn't quite agree with his optimism, the "kid" remark glancing off her as she was used to the comment from him. She was the youngest of the group by ten years, and where it had annoyed her upon first joining the team, she'd come to recognize it for the term of endearment it was meant to be.

"It's that, but it's not that. I'm just not satisfied with the result of the investigation. I know there's more to it, and the police aren't going to investigate any more. They're convinced they have it all figured out, but I know they're wrong."

"What about it makes you think there's more to it?" Bill asked. "I understand I don't know as much about it as you, but I've followed it in the papers, and it seems pretty straightforward. She was a nutjob."

So she laid it out for them. Beginning with her discovery of the chip, taking it to Casey, his research into how it functioned, her investigation into Mark Minsky's network, and taking it to the police. Once she got to the attack on her and the way Tessa had confessed, she had both the boys' full attention. She had to admit it was a crazy story. Unbelievable even though it had happened to her.

"So you see, I just don't think she could've pulled it off

on her own. Even if it was only a tool for keeping tabs on her boyfriends, which I still don't buy. The whole resolution is just too simple for such a complex device."

"But she could've made it," Phil said. "Technically, I mean. She had the skills, right?'

"She did," Cameron agreed. "But the scope of something like this is just too broad. Even if it had started that way, the implications of what a device like that could be used for would've been apparent. Especially for her. She was the VP of sales for SE. You can't tell me she didn't at least recognize the monetary value. And if she was as crazy in love and as desperate as everyone's making her out to be, she surely would've brought her idea to those guys. Wouldn't the idea have made her more attractive to them in her mind?"

Bill nodded. The most technical of their group, he would easily see where she was going. "I agree. So let's break it down. The cops have gone through all the data and found nothing to incriminate anyone else, correct?"

"Yes, and that's another thing that bothers me. Anyone with the ability to build and manage this kind of technology would never be stupid enough to leave a video that would convict them. So stupid. I think one of the others set her up to take the fall."

"I could see that," he acknowledged. "What you need is whatever Matt Rodriguez found that got him killed in the first place. Your assumption is he saved that data, and that's why he was killed."

"Yes," she agreed, getting more animated at finally having someone support her theory. "But the police are satisfied the killer got all the data when they wiped everything at SE and his cloud account. I think they're wrong. They only found one cloud account. His business account for SE. I guarantee he had a personal account. Hell, my mother has a personal cloud account, and she doesn't even know what the cloud is. There isn't any way a guy that technically astute didn't have a private backup. And if he found something that significant, I'm willing to bet he stored the answers there."

"Okay," Phil said, "so if he did have a cloud account or backups that no one knew about, where would it be? And how would you even begin to gain access to it?"

That made Cameron pause, reflecting on their morning. Silence descended over the table as she dug into her eggs Benedict. Usually, she'd have called Casey for any tech issues. He'd have no problem accessing someone's cloud account, assuming she could find it.

"I know a guy," Bill piped up after chewing a massive amount of the pancakes he'd stuffed in his mouth. "One of my dealers, he's really good with computers, and not always in an aboveboard way. I can see if he has a password program you could run that would access that account if you can find it. I'll call him today. I'll have him send it to me, and you can throw it on a flash drive."

That gave Cameron pause, not so much that he had access to something like that but the look on his face when he said it. "Um, is that something you've gotten from him before?" she asked hesitantly.

"During my divorce," he answered, his face turning red. "My ex tried to hide something about her affair and our finances, so I did a little kracking. Technically all legal since we were still married, but still, keep it to yourself."

She nodded and Phil laughed. Divorce was a common topic in this group. Turned out being a SmartTech sales rep wasn't a conducive occupation for marriage.

"Well, that solves one problem, but you still have to find it. There are a million cloud hosting services available. How are you going to narrow down which one it is? You can't test all of them. That would take forever," Phil stated.

"Especially if he didn't use his real name to register it. Then you're screwed," Bill chimed in.

That again brought quiet to the group, and they all thought about the problem while sipping on their Bloodys and tucking into the food.

"I just keep thinking about that T-shirt Casey bought me. You know, the one he got me after I got the tech team those 'I'm here because you broke something' shirts." They nodded and she continued. "It said 'There is no cloud, it's only someone else's computer.'"

"Well, that's technically true, " Bill answered. "But I don't see how that gets you any closer to knowing where he hosted his cloud account."

"It doesn't. I mean, not really, but in a roundabout way. I was thinking where he would've been when he opened an account. He went to MIT. Surely he had a cloud account there? All students would've. Maybe he kept that one? It's probably one of the most secure services you could get. "

Phil whistled. "That's a whole other level of kracking. Can your guy's program get into something like that?"

Bill nodded. "Shouldn't be that big of a difference. You have a better shot at it if you try to access it from their network rather than remoting in. Could you find his old MIT email address? It's probably the username. That or his student ID."

"I can get it," she stated confidently. "I did a ton of research on all of them when I was working with the police. They did too. I'm sure it's in some of those files."

"You still have the police files?" Phil asked.

"Well, some of the information was shared digitally. Can you blame me if I saved it all?" A slow smile crept onto her face thinking of what Will would say. "I put it in my cloud account."

Bill snorted, tomato juice slipping out of his mouth. "The irony, I love it." He cleaned the mess on his face, still chuckling to himself. "This means you'll have to take a trip up to Boston,.

"Yep, thought of that," she answered. "I can head up tomorrow and be at MIT first thing Monday morning. Should give me time to get in, do what I need to do, and get back to Jersey before my meeting with Steve. Can I crash at your place Sunday night? I'd rather not have any record of my trip."

He nodded. "Of course you can. You know you're always welcome. But maybe we're thinking about this a little too hard."

"How do you mean?" she asked.

"I just think we're making it harder than it has to be. He was a tech genius. Isn't it more rational to think he kept his own backups? His own server? And I've got to think it would be easier to break into his apartment instead of MIT. And if it's not there, you might be able to find some evidence of where it would be."

"Dude, you're the genius," Phil replied.

Nodding, Cameron agreed. "Good call. I've got his address in the files. Sending it to you both now. Oh fantastic, we've done projects in this building. Phil, can you log into the quote system and see if you can find any floor plans? Bill, can you go to the building website and get the apartment layouts? Let's see if we have anything that'll match up and give us what we need to get in. See if you can find what kind of locks they have."

"Can do," Bill replied. "What are you going to do about the cameras? You know this building has surveillance."

"I'm not worried about that. Let 'em record me. Buildings like that usually don't keep those recordings long. They write over them to save storage space. No one should notice I've been there. It's not like Matt's going to be coming home again. What I'm more worried about is getting past the doorman."

"That's easy," Phil chimed in. "Just follow somebody in. Pretend to be on your phone and walk a few paces behind a group. When you catch the doorman's eye, just point to the people in from of you like you're with them. Works like a charm."

Cameron raised her eyebrows at that. "Something you've done often?" Seemed like both the guys had some hidden secrets they were sharing today.

"Once or twice," he answered with a wry smile. "I'm on this," he said, resuming clicking away at his keyboard. "What are you going to do?"

"Me? I'm going to get us another round."

She signaled the waitress and did just that, and the three of them sat in their booth engaged with their screens.

"Found the lock manufacturer," Bill piped up. "This is cake. You just need a laser."

Cameron smiled as she remembered the tech support guys teaching them that hack. "That'd be awesome, but remember, he took his HTH out of his apartment. I don't think we can count on being able to get in that way. I think I'm going to go old school on this one."

"What? The makeup trick? You think that'll work?" Phil asked.

"No worries. I'll go with her," Ben answered.

"No! Nobody else is getting dragged into this. I made that mistake with Casey. I won't do it again." She looked at them both with exasperation and banged her head on the table a few times before finally resting it there. She looked up when she felt someone's hand brush against her hair.

"You got your hair in the syrup," Bill told her sympathetically. "I get it. I won't tag along, but I'm not leaving the city tonight with all this going on. I'll get a hotel close by and you can come by after. We'll look at the data together."

"Thank you, that'd be great," she replied, wiping the syrup out of her hair with a napkin. "But here's what worries me. If I'm right and Tessa wasn't acting alone, that means someone out there has probably come to the same conclusion I have, and they'd be looking for the data as well."

Phil shook his head. "I don't like the idea that someone could still be after you. That incident in the city was way too close for comfort. That scar on your face is proof enough of that. Why don't you just take this info to the police again? Make them listen to you?"

"They won't," she said confidently, flashing back to her lunch with Will. "It's easier for them to just brush it off. They have their killer, and that's enough for them. Also, any delay would make it more likely that whoever else is involved would be able to find it and wipe it before I can. I don't want to take that chance."

She could go now. Get in tonight and examine the data on Sunday. Better than rushing to her Monday meeting with Steve. Getting her job back was just as important, and she'd do better if she was fresh for the appointment.

"I should go now. Quit wasting time and just get it over with for good. Can you call your contact and get that program today?"

"No problem. I'll have it before we leave this place," he said confidently, getting back on his MacBook and phone.

She turned to Phil. "Keep this to yourself, please. With what happened to Casey, I don't know what I'd do if anything happened to either of you."

He smiled. "Of course. First rule of the Northeast sales team: what happens in team meetings stays in team meetings."

She laughed. "It means a lot that you believed me. I appreciate the support."

"Anytime."

"Got it," Bill announced and handed her a flash drive.

"Well, that was quick," Phil commented.

"He's a good dude, and I gave him a massive discount on his last lighting project, so he owed me one."

CHAPTER FORTY

DISCOVERY

SHE headed home after leaving the restaurant. She wanted
to up her look to match that of the luxury building so she'd
blend in easier, and she couldn't do it in her funeral clothes.
Plus, she wanted to drop her rental car off at her building.
The only unknown was how long the password program
would take to run. There were too many variables in this
plan for her to feel confident. Too many assumptions that
almost drove her crazy on the short subway ride to 59th
Street. Did the cloud account even exist? She had all his
personal account information from the police files, so she
had usernames to check. It was crazy how easy people
made it to get access to their data. But then again, that's
what had been at the root of all of this madness to begin
with, so she shouldn't have been surprised. After all, she
managed to break into the Minskys' house with very little
trouble. She could do this. Looked like her life of crime

was just getting started.

She called Bill as she was walking the two blocks from her subway stop to his building. "I'm here."

"Okay," he answered. "Be careful, don't take any risks, and call me as soon as you're out. I checked into a hotel by your place. Come right here when you've got it."

She saw a group walking up to the doors and her heart soared. Perfect timing.

She nodded at the doorman, who was conveniently distracted by a resident and some dry cleaning, and pointed to the group in front of her. He nodded back, and she hustled to get in the elevator with them. Phase one complete. She was nervous as hell. In her state of near panic, she started humming the *Mission Impossible* theme song in her head again, trying to once again soothe her anxiety as she exited the elevator and made her way down the corridor on Matt's floor. She passed a few apartments but not the one she was looking for. Finally, she found it. Luckily, it was the last unit at the end of the hall. She glanced back the way she had come to confirm she was alone. She couldn't see anyone. She was good to go.

Pulling a jar of some old powder foundation she'd found in the back of a drawer out of her purse, she knelt down to get a better look at the keypad. She could see smudges on the screen. Perfect, it hadn't been cleaned. She unscrewed the cap and poured a light layer of the powder over the face of the keypad, then took a deep breath and blew it all off. Peering intently at what remained she broke into a huge grin. Only four numbers had residue left. She knew he lived alone but was worried he may have given additional codes to cleaning staff and such. Looked like there was only one code. Having a four-number limit narrowed the possibilities exponentially. Four numbers, ten thousand possibilities.

She leaned against the wall next to the door, trying to affect a casual stance. *Nothing weird going on here, just waiting for a friend.* Pulling out her phone, she opened an app to get a list of all possible combinations. Ten thousand tries would take forever. Taking a minute to think, she then went in a different direction. Pulling up her cloud storage and opening the police files on Matt Rodriguez, she initiated a search on the digits she found. Bingo, parents' home address: 1430. Score. She'd get in on the first try.

This was too easy. Maybe she and Casey should've forgotten all of this a week ago and really tried to rob a bank. She seemed to have the aptitude for it.

With one more quick glance down the hallway confirming she was alone, she keyed the code into the touch panel and hit the check mark. The lock disengaged. She was in.

She opened the door and silently let herself in, closing it behind her and reengaging the lock. She made her way by the moonlight filtering through the large open windows in his living room and looked around. It was a beautiful apartment, if sparsely furnished. Gleaming hardwood floors throughout told her he had a maid. The space was mostly open except for the standard bachelor leather couch and big TV. No clutter, so he was neat. Open to the kitchen and a dining area. She didn't bother turning on any lights as she made her way down the hallway; there was enough light from the windows to see perfectly. She was having flashbacks to Mark Minsky's house. Walking in a stranger's house, opening doors looking for electronics.

First door closet, second half bath. She hit pay dirt on the third. What was probably meant to be the second bedroom was a home office. Computer on the table and electronics stacked neatly on shelves covering both walls. Cables in plastic bins. She could've been in any of her customers' workrooms.

Her nerves faded as she sat down at the computer, at home in her natural environment. It booted up quickly, and she immediately saw the icon on the homepage for his login.

Letting that go for the time being, she followed the cables connecting to the terminal and found what she was looking for. Servers. Three of them. Looked like Matt did store his own backups. Now to see if they were connected or if she'd have to go in directly.

She went back to the computer and noted the time and realized she'd only been in the apartment for two minutes. This was going well. Now she just had to hold it together for the hard part. She pulled the thumb drive out of her pocket and inserted it into the PC. Clicking onto the access screen, she began running the password program. This was the part that worried her. It could take one minute, or it could take hours to crack the password on his computer. So she waited.

But waiting was not Cameron's strong suit. No one would ever call her a patient person. As the minutes ticked by, she almost drove herself crazy imagining what would happen if she were caught. She'd go to jail for sure. Breaking and entering. Computer hacking. That was probably pretty bad, but the guy was dead, so did it matter?

After ten minutes ticked by, Cameron had bitten her fingernails down to the quick. After fifteen minutes, she was ready to say screw it and run out the door. Finally, after twenty minutes, when she was almost out the door, the program finished running. She was in.

Walking to the machine, she felt like she was in a haze. She immediately located the directory to see all attached drives. They were there. Three external storage units. *Take that, Detective.* They did exist. Now to see if there was any info regarding the HomeTech Hub on there. Opening the files, she blessed Matt Rodriguez for being an organized guy. Everything in his account was divided into folders and subfolders, and his subfolders had subfolders. It was beautifully laid out. She found what she was looking for in seconds.

There was a file marked with last Friday's date, the night Matt was killed, titled "HTH Anomaly." She wanted more than anything to open the file and finally get answers, but she knew this wasn't the place. She checked the storage on the thumb drive. Seeing it had a terabyte of storage available, she mentally thanked Bill and began copying the files. She also logged onto the internet, opened her cloud account, and began transferring everything stored in Matt's cloud account there too. A little backup never hurt.

The downloads were moving rapidly, but she was still anxious to get out of there as she waited. Things had gone smoothly to this point, but any second she knew things could change.

In the next moment, they did. She noticed the light from the hallway disappear as an object moved in front of the doorway. She swiveled in the chair when she heard someone enter the room.

CHAPTER FORTY-ONE

I TOLD YOU SO

"HOLY shit, it was you" was all that came out of her mouth when she saw the man standing inside the door. He shut it behind him when he entered, and now she was trapped. Blocked in this room, in the dark, with a man she was pretty sure was going to kill her.

"Bet you thought it would've been Trey," Brandon Reece said as he took a step farther into the room.

"I did," she admitted. "To be honest, I thought you might have known about it, but I didn't expect you to show up here. How'd you find me?"

"Trey was a little nervous after he spoke to Mark about how you discovered our little project and told the police. Pretty pissed too. You caused us a lot of problems."

"Sorry," she said sarcastically, "but you killed my friend."

"No I didn't," he answered, moving another step closer

to her. "Tessa hired someone to kill your friend. But back to why I'm here. Trey and I weren't satisfied that Matteo hadn't stored the information somewhere else. Probably just like you were. And he knew the police couldn't figure it out. After Tessa's confession, they were satisfied. The ADA certainly was with all the publicity and an open-and-shut case. With video, no less! But after meeting you in the elevator at the police station, Trey began to worry about you. I mean, you were the only one involved who had enough technical knowledge to question anything. So, Trey hacked your phone. When we saw you were headed to this building, it all came together, and Trey realized what you'd come here for. So, I decided to meet you here. See what you found."

She didn't bother to answer that snarky statement. He'd slowly been moving closer to her as he'd been speaking, and while it was a large room, he was closing the space between them pretty quickly. She was getting really scared. She couldn't bank on someone hearing her if she screamed—surely in a building like, this they had pretty good insulation—so it looked like she'd have to figure another way out of this. She'd been glancing around for anything to use as a weapon, but there wasn't anything obvious. Why couldn't Matt have been into baseball or something? Would it have hurt for him to have a bat laying nearby? The best she could come up with was the keyboard. If you brained someone with that, it could do some damage. At least enough to get around him and out the door. It would take a few seconds, but if she hit him hard enough, she might have enough time.

The computer behind her beeped. The download was complete. She met his eyes and knew he knew it too.

"I guess you got what you came for, huh? Your proof?"

"I don't know yet. I haven't had a chance to look through the files."

"But you got it. That's pretty good. Matteo wasn't a slouch when it came to security. That's why we recruited him for the project."

"Why do you call him Matteo and everyone else called him Matt?"

Keep him talking. Just buy a little more time.

The question seemed to stump him, and he stopped moving forward while he answered. "I didn't care for the guy. Trey liked him a lot, and Tessa messed around with him, but she messed around with everyone. He wasn't our kind of people. After Trey hired him, he was always around, like Trey's freaking puppy or something. He was a necessary evil to me, not a friend. We needed his device as a delivery system. Trey saw the value in it. It didn't mean much to me when he finally caught on to what we were doing and he had to die. He was way too moral to go along with our plan. You know he told Trey? Like he wouldn't know about it. He wanted to have a meeting, pull all the units from the shelves. The kid signed his own death warrant if you ask me."

"But you didn't kill him?" she asked.

"Nope, the video's legit. Tessa did it. I would've—hell, I wanted to—but with a few sweet words, Trey had Tessa all wound up and ready to do his bidding. He could've made her do anything. I still can't believe she's taking the fall for him. Bitches are stupid. He doesn't even love her."

He began to inch closer to her again and was getting close to striking distance. She knew the conversation was almost over when he reached into his pocket to pull out a wicked-looking knife.

"And that's why I have to die too?" she asked. "Because bitches are stupid?"

"Pretty much, yeah. Plus, you think we're rich now? Wait until we get this up and running," he replied, looking at the knife and then back at her. "This is going to be messy, which is disappointing, but a gun would be too loud. You should've let it go, but bitches like you, man, you sure are stupid."

And with that final barb, he lunged at her. Cameron had been waiting for that move, and in one motion she stood, grabbed the keyboard from the desk, and swung it at his head. She immediately realized her mistake as she felt her momentum jerk backward. It wasn't a wireless keyboard; she was being pulled back by the cord. She did not anticipate that. She'd assumed that was too old-school for somebody like Matt.

The change in momentum was enough to make her lose her balance and send her careening backward, falling toward the desk. But it must have been enough of a change to throw off Brandon's aim, because when she felt the knife enter her body, it was on her side. Probably not where he was aiming. She hit her head on the desk behind her, her feet flying up in the air as she fell, landing an awkward kick to Brandon's knee. Then she crumpled to the ground.

Her head hurt as she tried to assess her situation from her position on the ground almost underneath the desk she'd been using. Brandon was on the ground a few feet away, holding his knee and rolling on the floor. The knife was on the rug next to her. He didn't get enough leverage to lodge it into her during her acrobatic fall. As she reached down to the pain in her side, her hand came away wet. He still did some damage. She reached over and picked up the knife with her bloody hand, then pushed herself to her feet. She had trouble staying upright but did her best to veer around him as she headed for the door.

"You fucking bitch!" Brandon screamed from his place on the floor. He was shuffling around and trying to crawl after her. "Get back here."

Yeah right, like I'm going back.

She kept hobbling forward, the door blurring in and out of focus. She must have messed up her head, or else the stab wound in her side was worse than she thought. Maybe she was losing too much blood. It didn't matter either way. She was determined to get out of the apartment and get help before he could get it together and come for her again. She didn't know if she had it in her to use the knife and stab another person, and she hoped she didn't have to find out.

She made it to the hallway, leaning against it as she moved, smearing blood all over the white walls. What felt like a short distance to the front door on her entry now felt like miles, the pain scorching with each step. With each little shuffle, she got closer to the exit, and she could hear Brandon behind her, moving, cursing, trying to come after her.

She took a quick pause about halfway down to catch her breath and chanced a glance back. *Stupid, you never look back, you just keep running.* Rule number one in every horror movie she'd ever seen. But she saw Brandon on the floor, head poking through the doorway into the hall as he tried to crawl after her.

She turned and resumed her slow staggered pace to the front door. Finally, after what felt like hours, she made it. She was spent. She had used all her energy getting there. She pressed herself against the front door, hand on the handle, and when it opened, she fell through with it.

Bracing herself for the impact hitting the floor would cause, she was surprised when someone caught her. Looking up, she saw a familiar face.

"I…." She tried to talk, but her field of vision was getting narrower, and vertigo was starting to creep in. "I… I told you so."

Then she promptly passed out.

CHAPTER FORTY-TWO

NOW IT'S OVER

CAMERON came to again in what she slowly realized was a hospital room. Sunlight was streaming through the window, so she felt sure she'd missed a lot of hours somewhere. She took stock of herself—all limbs accounted for and movable. Most of her pain was localized to her right side and her stomach, where she assumed she'd been stabbed. She also had the dull thudding of a slight headache, probably from where she whacked her head on the table. She glanced to her right and saw Bill sitting in the chair beside her bed.

"Hey," she croaked. Her voice was hoarse and her throat dry.

"Hey," he said, scooting closer. "You're awake."

"Yep, and it appears I still have all my body parts, so that feels like a win."

"You scared the shit out of us, Cameron. When I didn't hear back from you after a few hours, I started calling and nothing. Eventually, I had Phil track down the detective from the NYPD that you worked with. We got his number, and he told us where you were."

"Detective Justus? How did he know where I was?"

"You don't remember? He was there last night. He found you. He arrested Brandon Reece after you took him down."

Cameron stretched her memory, but she had no recollection of Will from last night. "I remember Brandon doing his villain monologue. I remember falling, but nothing after that."

"It's not surprising. You took quite a bump on the head and got a nasty concussion. But you're going to be okay. The stab wound in your side was the main thing. You lost a lot of blood and had to have a transfusion. They stitched you up, and there was no major organ damage. You should be out of here in a day or two. I don't think you'll be ready to be alone for a while, so I'll stay at your place until you recover fully."

"You said I took Brandon down? How did that happen?"

Bill's smile grew wider, and she could tell he was trying to hold in a laugh. "It was fantastic. Matt had security cameras. I've seen the footage." His laugh grew full out at that.

"What? What's so funny?"

Bill could barely get through the explanation, he was laughing so hard. "You did this acrobatic… thing. I don't know, you… like…." And then he made some insane gesture, flinging his hands around. "No, seriously, you tried to hit him with a keyboard, but it was plugged into the desktop you were using. I guess you put a lot of leverage into it, because when the cable caught, you did this... this... well, you launched into the air and nailed him in the knee. On the way down is when you cracked your head on the desk."

"A kick to the knee took him down? No way. That guy was fit."

His expression then took a serious tone. All hint of laughter was gone. "You were really lucky. He had an old rugby injury, and that was his bad knee. If that hadn't happened, you would've been dead. It was another two minutes before the detective showed up."

Cameron was stunned. What a crazy series of events.

"So, it's Sunday?" she asked. "I guess that means I'm going to miss my meeting with Steve. That's just great. I'm sure he'll love this twist. Freakin' Steve."

"It'll be okay. You're going to be fine. The rest of it is just semantics," he said, squeezing her hand. "It could've been so much worse if the detective wasn't there."

"Why was he there? I still don't understand what happened."

"Do you want me to get him?" he asked. "He's been waiting here all night."

She nodded, and Bill left the room. She struggled to find the controls for the bed, but eventually she did and raised the bed to a sitting position she could tolerate even with the pain radiating from her side. She reached over and grabbed a glass of water from the bedside table, wincing as she took a small sip through the straw. Then she noticed Will standing in the doorway to her room.

"Hey," she greeted him.

"Hey," he replied. "How're you feeling?"

"I've had better days."

"I'm sure. Your friend Bill says you're having a little trouble putting together what happened last night?"

She nodded. "I don't understand how you found us. Don't get me wrong, I'm grateful. Just confused."

"Well, I guess it started when you left me at the restaurant on Friday." She winced a bit at the hurt look on his face. *That was surprising. I didn't think I'd affected him that much,* she thought as he continued.

"I thought about what you said, and you were so sure, so convinced, I began to wonder if maybe there wasn't more to it as well, so I followed you after the funeral. I figured you'd still be looking for the answers, and maybe if you were, then someone else was as well. I admit it threw me for a loop when you went to Matt's apartment, but I knew you were on to something when I saw Brandon Reece walk in not too far behind you. I wish I would've followed you instead of him. When we went into the building, I lost him for a bit getting in the door. He followed someone in, but the doorman stopped me. That's why I was late getting to you. I'm so sorry I wasn't there sooner. I could've stopped him from getting to you."

"Don't worry about it. It all worked out. Did you get the flash drive?"

"We did. The tech guys are going through all the information as we speak, but you were right. They were all in on it. We have enough there to arrest and convict Trey Howell."

"What about Brandon?"

"Him too. He's here in the hospital as well. Handcuffed to his bed with an officer on guard."

She nodded, sleepy from whatever the doctors had given her. "So that's it, then. It's all over?"

"It's all over," he agreed, reaching out to hold her hand. "I'm so sorry I didn't believe you. You were right, about everything. It was Trey's plan from the beginning. Tessa and Brandon were both in on it, and they kept it from Matt for as long as they could. They all planned his murder, banking on the party as cover for all of them. They were beta testing the data retrieval capabilities on themselves before they were going to try to market it. Who knows who they thought they were going to sell it to? Our government, someone else's, a private company. We don't have all the details on that yet, and we may never know for sure, but at the very least, the project has been shut down. We've recovered all the chips, and Tessa, Brandon, and Trey are going away for a very long time."

"You can't put the genie back in the box," she said, sounding a little loopier than before. The painkillers they had her on must have been on a time release, or maybe that was what was in her IV. "Now that it's out there, someone else will figure it out too."

"Maybe so, but that's not for us to worry about. There have been some government suits sniffing around. I'm pretty sure they'll want to talk to you too. My guess is they'll take custody of all the materials, and it'll be like it never happened."

"Shh," she said, putting a finger to her lips. "Don't tell them about my cloud account."

That made him chuckle. He pushed her hair out of her face and whispered, "I would never." He smiled. "Get some rest. I'll be here when you wake up."

He leaned down and softly kissed her lips.

Well, she thought as she drifted off, *that was interesting*.

ACKNOWLEDGMENTS

To the crew at Hot Tree Self-Publishing, thanks for everything. You made this possible.

Shout out to my family, Mom, Dad, Andy, Graham, and Kristen. Wouldn't be anywhere without you.

To Ben and Ken, how did I get so lucky to get partnered up with you two? I've been honored to have your friendship for the last ten years. I've learned more from you than I can say. I can't tell you how much you mean to me. Sorry for telling tales, but some are too hilarious not to share. I left out most of the good stuff. Love you both.

To my Friday night poker group. Thanks for letting me use your names. Kim, Mike, Nick, Mark, Jay, Ed, Wayne, Al, Dennis, Richard, and Jimmy. You guys are the best.

To Eytan, Scott, Chris, and Tayt, thank god Ohio ended up in the northeast. To Clint for the advice.

To Nancy, it's amazing to have a friend who holds you accountable and supports you unconditionally. You're one of a kind.

To Chris Perkins, thanks for all the "teaching moments." Marla Suttenberg, who taught me a badass woman could be a badass boss and look good doing it. Cory, for letting me kill him; it's a shame about the polar bears. Fred Bargetzi, who talked to me and listened to me like my voice was important when I was a newbie. You have no idea how much your kindness stayed with me.

To Toby, Patrick, Lainie, Narayan, Mark, Kathryn Cordina, Ellen, and Marcia. To Delia, Tricia, Sandy, Abby, Maria, Liz, Tara, Melissa, Candice, Clancy, Roseanne, Tom, Hatcher, Casey, Turner, Michelle, Bryan Celli, Keith, Marcus, Yohanna, Glenn, Jon, Carl, Manish, Ray, Alex, Justin, Dominick, Charlie, Doug, Andrew, Rich, Maria, and every member of the swirl family I forgot to list. I didn't forget you, and I'll never forget how much better I am for having known you.

To the guys at B&W, thanks for the motivation to make me want to be one of the guys who sat at the table.

To Tony for giving me my start.

To all my dealers, past, present, and future. I love you all. Before you say anything about the tech in this book, I'M AWARE! It's fiction; sometimes you've got to get creative.

And finally, for Bob. I wish you were here to see this. I know no one would've been prouder than you.

ABOUT THE AUTHOR

Kat has worked for eighteen years in sales in the AV industry, her love for technology starting early with her first computer, a Commodore64 at age six. She loved it until she realized you could put a magnet to the screen and it made pretty colors.

Kat spends a lot of her time traveling. She's been to forty-six states and lived in six. She loves yoga, poker, sports, and all things technology. Her dreams are to one day stop travelling so much and be able to own a dog and to be the first woman to win the World Series of Poker Main Event.

Made in the USA
Monee, IL
25 January 2021